Dear America

The Diary of
Emma Simpson

When Will This
Cruel War Be Over?

Barry Denenberg

SCHOLASTIC INC. ◆ NEW YORK

For my own lovely Emma

Copyright © 1996 by Barry Denenberg

The Library of Congress has cataloged the earlier hardcover edition as follows:
Denenberg, Barry. When will this cruel war be over? : the Civil War diary of Emma
Simpson, Gordonsville, Virginia, 1864 / by Barry Denenberg. p. cm. — (Dear America;
1) Summary: The diary of a fictional fourteen-year-old girl living in Virginia, in which
she describes the hardships endured by her family and friends during one year of the
Civil War. ISBN 0-590-22862-5 (alk. paper) 1. United States.—History—Civil War,
1861–1865—Juvenile fiction. [1. United States.—History—Civil War, 1861–1865—Fiction. 2.
Diaries—Fiction. 3. Virginia—Fiction.] I. Title. II. Series. PZ7.D4135Wh 1996 [Fic]—dc20
95-25540 CIP AC

Trade Paper-Over-Board edition ISBN 978-0-545-27598-9
Reinforced Library edition ISBN 978-0-545-27944-4

10 9 8 7 6 5 4 3 2 1   11 12 13 14 15

The text type was set in ITC Legacy Serif.
The display type was set in Centaur MT.
Book design by Kevin Callahan

Printed in the U.S.A.   23
This edition first printing, April 2011

Gordonsville,
Virginia

1863

Times gone by

Wednesday, December 23, 1863

Brother Cole returned home today.

I cannot fully convey the pain that pierced my heart as Nelson and Amos carried his coffin from the cart.

Mother is inconsolable — her hopes so recently raised by the intelligence that he was recovering from his wounds in Richmond.

We received word that he was on lookout duty late one evening when a ball from a Yankee sharpshooter's rifle wounded him in the chest. His condition, although serious, was not thought to be life threatening. We were told that when he was well enough to travel he would be given a furlough and returned home.

Only two weeks later we learned that, while recuperating in the hospital, he died from pneumonia.

As I write this I wonder how I can remain so

calm. Perhaps the full knowledge of what has happened to our family has not been wholly realized.

What words can I use to express our profound grief? How can I adequately describe the apprehension, fear, hope and, finally, despair that has filled our days?

As if it were not enough to learn of his suffering, what solace are we to find in knowing that he met his demise not in glorious battle defending our beloved land, but was touched by the hands of fate in such a tragic manner?

Mother urges me to trust in the Lord, for He is our protector.

Brother Cole is safe in heaven, now. Surely the Lord is with him. He was a good son and a gentle brother. I fear we shall not see his kind again.

Friday, December 25, 1863

There will be no Christmas celebration this year.

My thoughts dwell on times gone by. My memories beckon to me, pulling me back, reminding me at every turn of how our lives used to be, reminding me of Christmases past.

Even Father, who usually tolerated no variation of his arduous daily duties, considered Christmas a special time. He and Brother Cole would go with Nelson to choose a proper tree, which Father insisted be put up as early as possible so that we could decorate it appropriately and enjoy it for the longest possible time.

The house would be a beehive of activity for weeks before.

Mother was even more occupied than usual: seeing to it that everything was just so, supervising the Negroes, talking to Dolphy about readying all the beautiful silk and satin dresses we would be wearing — we all dressed with such care then — to Denise about preparing the food, and Iris about the endless list of housekeeping chores.

The guest rooms on the second and third floors had to be put in perfect "apple-pie order," as Iris called it. Everything was washed, swept, dusted, cleaned, and polished until each room sparkled.

The house was filled with the merry sounds of loved ones and warmed by a feeling of hospitality that lightened the heart. The children gleefully anticipating their gifts — candy and toys, a wagon with horse attached, a monkey in a box, a hobbyhorse, dolls, and diaries.

The hams, turkeys, mutton, and bacon were brought from the smokehouse by the Negroes, and the tables piled high with pies, cakes, cookies, and candies.

It seems only yesterday that we anxiously awaited the arrival of Uncle Benjamin, Aunt Caroline, and Cousin Rachel from Richmond. Father enjoyed Uncle Benjamin's company immensely, taking out the chessboard immediately upon his arrival. Aunt Caroline is so much like Mother, both in appearance and manner — one would think they were twins. And Cousin Rachel, whom I have known nearly all my life, grew dearer to me with each visit. O how glorious was their arrival, made all the more glorious by the knowledge that they would remain with us to greet the New Year. There was so much to talk about; those days seemed to just fly by.

Could it be only three years ago that Father, Mother, Brother Cole, and I stood on the front porch greeting the constant stream of friends, neighbors, and relatives arriving to celebrate the Christmas season? I can see the scene so clearly in my mind's eye, as house servants darted in and out, attending to the gift-laden carriages, making sure that all the guests were nicely settled in their rooms.

Those visits were the most joyous memories of my life. Alas, now they are only that, memories.

I can remember that Christmas Eve, after our sleigh ride — how gloriously Mother sang hymns for us that night, while Aunt Caroline accompanied her on the piano. Mother has such a melodious voice, and she and Aunt Caroline are the picture of harmony.

Cousin Rachel had to be coaxed for quite a time but she finally agreed to grace us with her delightful flute playing. She, like Mother and Aunt Caroline, is so talented.

I wish I were as gifted as they, but I am afraid that I am not musically inclined.

They each have such beautiful, wavy brown hair — I am envious. I wish mine looked more like theirs, rather than this common, straight, dark hair that I, like Brother Cole, seem to have inherited from Father.

All of us drinking eggnog as Father offered a toast to everyone's lifelong health and happiness.

And O how hard it was to wait for Christmas morning. Brother Cole and I would wake everyone at dawn, eager to see what was in our stockings.

I can still remember the surprised look on Cousin Rachel's face when she unwrapped her gift, revealing the two lively, little white rabbits that she immediately Christened Agnes and Annie. That night we stayed up until the early hours of the morning, talking and feeding them apples and cabbage leaves.

And Cousin Rachel was such a delight to

converse with. I know I tend to be on the quiet side. Mother accuses me of being much too serious and thinks that Cousin Rachel is a proper antidote for me, since she is such a chatterbox. Mother is, of course, correct in her supposition, for I am truly comforted when Cousin Rachel is around to entertain me with her endless conversation—she has an opinion on everything

Everyone seemed so happy then. How could I know that would be the last time I would see Uncle Benjamin? How could I know it would be the last Christmas we would all celebrate together?

1863 was the most dismal year of my life.

The house seems so empty now, for indeed it is. Father has been gone for over two years. And my dear, sweet Brother Cole is in the kingdom of the Lord.

Once it wasn't that way.

Now our land is in a distressing state. Our struggle with the Yankees is, they say, going poorly, even after two years of this infernal fighting.

Friday, January 1, 1864

I have decided upon my resolutions for the New Year. I have always had the habit of writing down my resolutions and referring to them from time to time throughout the year.

Those I made in years past seem so childish: wash my hair more, take better care of my appearance, watch sweets, tend to the horses, rise earlier in the morning.

This year I have decided to concentrate on fewer areas in the hope that I can be more successful.

I have resolved to faithfully keep my diary, which was begun at Mother's suggestion. She hoped it might help develop my writing skills and improve my penmanship.

I strive to take my time — although there is so much I want to say that sometimes my pen flies in my hand and I have to remind myself to take care.

My only other resolution, which is truthfully the most important one, is to try and help Mother more. I must confess, I have felt overwhelmed many times over the past two years. I fear I have been more of a burden to Mother than a help. So much has fallen on her shoulders. This coming year I vow that she can depend on me more.

My most fervent prayer is that 1864 will be a happier year, although I do not see anything on the horizon that would support that hope. I trust that the Lord will provide.

One does not know what to expect these days

Sunday, January 3, 1864

The thermometer reached only seven degrees today. There were icicles hanging from the house and the trees — and the milk freezes if left exposed. It was so cold we did not attend church.

It has been difficult without Father.

Father and Mother always had their responsibilities strictly defined, unless Mother required his assistance with the more troublesome Negroes. Father saw to the farm and the fieldwork while Mother saw to the house and the house servants — everything ran like clockwork. My world seemed so safe and secure then. I thought it would always remain that way.

Now all responsibilities have fallen to Mother. She has done her best, but Father's lengthy absence has shown us how various were his tasks. I fear that Mother cannot replace him in all areas, try as she might.

Nelson has been a great help to Mother. He, along with Amos and Iris, is proving to be one of our most reliable Negroes. He has helped Mother see to it that the tobacco, corn, and other crops are properly cared for and that the horses and livestock are tended to. These tasks had become a time-consuming part of Mother's day. As always, Amos assists Mother with her garden.

Our Negroes, bless them, mind Mother as they always have and I cannot think of one instance in which they have not helped in every way.

Still, I think they miss Father's understanding but firm guiding hand. When Father was home contentment and order reigned supreme. Father always treated our Negroes with compassion — using force only when called for.

There is constant talk now, especially by Mr. Garlington and Doctor Harris, of a growing spirit of rebelliousness among the Negroes in the area. I have not seen any evidence of this. However, one does not know what to expect these days.

Monday, January 4, 1864

We are so isolated here — seldom seeing the number of visitors we used to, and I miss that very much.

Mrs. Broyles and her daughters, Lily and Lucy, came by today. Although they are a year and two younger than me — Lily is the elder — they are quite pleasant company. Both Broyles boys have gone off to fight the war.

Last fall Mother told me that Mrs. Broyles thought I was a proper influence on her two girls, and Mother hoped I would do my best to be courteous to them. I do find them both sweet and kind, although it is no use talking to them about anything serious. I hope I am not being too harsh — Mother says I am too hard on people.

I told Mother it would be fine if she invited them to see the beautiful new colt that Falla had just given birth to. Falla was named such because when she was born Amos said she would "falla" him everywhere.

They helped me feed Falla some corn and care for the new colt. They seemed to take to the horses right away, and I think they enjoyed themselves.

Later I suggested that we all go riding. I rode Little, who will not let anyone but me ride her, and Lily rode Plum. Lucy began by riding Boy, who, however, proved too much for her because he enjoys galloping and can be skittish. Lily manages the horses better so I had her ride Boy and put Lucy on Plum.

We all had a delightful time, and that night ate apples, which we baked on the hearth, and roasted eggs, which we cut in half so we could remove the yolks and fill the cavity with salt. We also helped Denise make ice cream and molasses candy in the kitchen.

During this more recent visit, Mrs. Broyles and Mother talked at length in the parlor. Mother told me later that Mrs. Broyles feels quite alone. They have not seen a white face for nearly a month. She is quite concerned about her two boys, whose decision to join the war has left her in a dreadful state. She lost her husband at Gettysburg last July. She learned of his tragic death when she saw his name in the newspaper's casualty report. Mother counsels her that the Lord will not forsake those who put their trust in Him.

The story takes me far away from my own troubles

Tuesday, January 5, 1864

I have decided to commence reading again. I read only one book last year, which is quite odd for me, and was due to my melancholy state. The one book was *Emma*, by Jane Austen, which Mother gave me for my birthday. It was inscribed: "To my own lovely Emma." I told Mother I hoped she didn't think I was anything like that Emma. She is forever poking her nose into everybody's affairs and paying too little attention to her own. Mother laughed when I told her this and assured me that she did not think that about me. She thought only that it would make an appropriate birthday gift because her name was the same as mine, and that I might like the story, which I most assuredly did.

Mother has been insistent that things remain, whenever possible, as they were.

As before the war, Mother and I breakfast alone, after she has spoken with Iris, Denise, Dolphy, and Nelson. As I mentioned, the time she spends with Nelson is necessitated by Father's absence. So we begin our day by eight o'clock — an hour later than usual.

After Iris serves us biscuits and apple butter for breakfast, we read from the Bible — which mother is quite adamant about — and then we begin my studies. I do not care much for arithmetic, geometry, rhetoric, or French lessons, preferring the time we spend on reading.

Although I think Mother is, at times, concerned with my lack of attention to some of my studies, we both take great delight in my reading list, which Mother attends to with great care. Books are becoming quite difficult to obtain, but our library, which Mother takes as much pride in as her garden, affords a wealth of possibilities. Mother has composed quite a respectable list for me.

I do love reading so and intend to devour everything on Mother's list this year. I know she was disappointed by my inattentiveness last year, and the great amount of time I spent idly in my room.

Each morning, after Mother reads a chapter aloud, we discuss the book we are reading. We began this year with *Wuthering Heights*, which, I must confess, I am having some difficulty with.

For one thing, I am, at times, confused by the characters. Perhaps I am foolish, but I do not understand how anyone can be as dark and troubled as Heathcliff. Nor do I understand why he would care so much for Catherine, who seems quite frivolous to me and unworthy of all that attention.

I am, however, enjoying *Wuthering Heights*, for the story takes me far away from my own troubles.

Wednesday, January 6, 1864

Try as I might, I cannot seem to stop thinking about times past. The long walks, the buggy rides into town, the dances and fancy balls after which we would feast on cake, strawberries, and ice cream, the sparkling conversation, the laughter and the merriment — there is none of that now.

Although I have vowed to keep my mind on the tasks at hand and not dwell on the past, as I did last year, so many little things remind me of the way things once were.

Just this morning I was fixing my hair — which seems to vex me no matter what I do — and I realized I was using Cousin Rachel's comb, the one she lost last summer.

That, now that I think of it, was the last time we went into town to shop for new dresses at Mr. Breckinridge's store. Even then there was little to choose from. Mother says we have the Yankee blockade to thank for that. Despite Mr. Breckinridge's diminished selection, Cousin Rachel and I spent sufficient time making our choices and then rushed home to try them on in preparation for dinner.

That night Cousin Rachel and I drank, I think, too much strong tea and were up till three o'clock in the morning talking about personal matters, the war, and marriage — which has become one of Cousin Rachel's favorite topics. I can only attribute this to the fact that she is three years older than me.

The next day we went riding at dawn in order to avoid the heat of the day. Cousin Rachel insisted on riding Sultan, although I cautioned her against it. Sultan can be as stubborn as a mule when he sets his mind to it. And the more he is whipped the more stubborn he becomes, turning every which way and moving off at whatever pace suits him. Of course, he is a superior animal. In the open field I have never ridden a horse that can best him. He flies like the wind.

It was a beautiful morning. The ground was covered with dew and there wasn't a sound to be heard above the horses' hooves.

Just when we were about to return home, Cousin Rachel's comb fell out of her hair. When she jumped to the ground to retrieve it, Sultan jerked the bridle out of her hand and made for the house, happily riderless, his mane flying in the wind. Cousin Rachel immediately took off after him, her now loosened hair also flying behind her.

I followed slowly behind, laughing at the scene unfolding before me. When we finally reached the house, the Negroes working in the field stopped to watch the spectacle. Sultan had been put back in his stall, from which he stared balefully at us, although I thought I could detect a twinkle in his eye.

That night we regaled everyone with the story of Sultan and the lost hair comb which, I realized this morning, I had retrieved, but never given back to Cousin Rachel.

It gives me some welcome relief to allow my mind to dwell on those pleasing memories of the past. Alas, there are, all too often, frequent reminders of sadder memories. The saddest are those of Brother Cole.

Each morning I am reminded of the competition between Father and Brother Cole to see who would be the first to wake in the morning. Brother Cole played the game, I must say, with little success.

Iris, too, took great delight in watching the two of them, as she would gleefully report to Mother and me on those rare occasions when Father would descend the stairs to find his son sitting in his customary seat at the breakfast table.

Iris brought us near to tears trying to imitate Father's shock, followed by his heartfelt laugh and Brother Cole's beaming smile.

Aunt Caroline and Cousin Rachel's company has been the only thing that truly takes my mind from the trials of the past two years.

I was gravely disappointed that they were unable to join us this Christmas, due to the situation in Richmond and the general fear of traveling that has caused so much consternation in the area.

My diary has become my true friend

Saturday, January 9, 1864

My diary has become my true friend.

Expressing my thoughts in writing, especially during these dark days that have descended on our sunny land, is a great comfort to me.

Sunday, January 10, 1864

Attended church today. Amos placed a warm brick and extra blankets in the carriage to keep Mother and me as comfortable as possible. It is snowing lightly.

I washed my hair today.

Monday, January 11, 1864

I wonder if anyone will ever think me presentable — although I know this is a silly question to ask, especially at this time. I certainly hope I am not becoming vain, but it is useless to try and put these thoughts aside once they arise. I wonder if ugly people are able to find other ugly people and are actually attracted to them — although I am not so foolish as to think I am ugly. At times I feel quite pleased with myself, especially if I am wearing a pretty dress and my hair is done in a fashion I think is flattering.

I wonder if pretty girls feel pretty all the time?

I know that all of this sounds quite foolish but I feel it is better to write in my diary — where no one will ever see it — than speak to anyone about such foolishness.

Wednesday, January 13, 1864

I never realized how happy I was until this war besieged our land.

The moon had never shone as brightly

Monday, January 18, 1864

I wonder if I will ever fall in love. He will have to be someone whom I feel is worthy. I must confess I do have an image in my heart. I do have a weakness for beauty. I care nothing of what others might think, but I do desire to gaze on a face I find pleasing. Should I be different? I am not sure I can be.

Of course he must have other characteristics. He must be intelligent and possess a sense of honor. I could never marry anyone I did not respect. The most important thing is to be sure you love the one you marry with your whole heart.

It is hard for me to believe that a year ago, at this time, Tally and I had not even met.

I miss him more and more as the days go by.

Last year, in July, when Aunt Caroline gave birth to Baby Elizabeth and we learned of Uncle

Benjamin's tragic death, Mother decided we should make the journey to Richmond, despite the dangers. The journey, although arduous, was without incident and we arrived exhausted, but happy to see our beloved relatives.

Early the next morning Cousin Rachel had the carriages brought around and we spent most of the day in town. Richmond is so much larger than Gordonsville; I felt quite overwhelmed.

That evening we chose our dresses — I wore the one with the wreath of roses and a white lily in my hair — for the reception that Aunt Caroline was giving in honor of Baby Elizabeth's birth.

One boy, whose name I cannot quite remember, which is no wonder, boldly introduced himself to me.

Like most boys, he seemed to take great pride in misunderstanding everything I said, twisting it this way and that and politely pointing out precisely where my thinking was in error, although I honestly do not recall talking about anything that warranted such attention.

There is nothing that troubles me more than people who go out of their way to criticize everything you say, holding each sentence under a magnifying glass and repeating it back to you in a completely unrecognizable fashion.

Like most boys, he was more interested in debate than discussion, more concerned with the sound of his own words than what others were saying. He employed what I can only call a kind of false voice when he was about to orate on a particular subject.

I do not know what it is about boys that causes them to think this behavior impresses girls but, frankly, it vexes me quite a bit.

I endured it for as long as I could—it seemed as if we had been chatting for an eternity—finally excusing myself by telling him that I had to attend to a private matter, which, I could see, put him in quite a state.

I slowly ferried my way through the gathering, which had, by now, grown quite sizable.

I badly needed some air, and I hoped the portico would provide some. Before I arrived at my destination Aunt Caroline beckoned to me. She introduced me to a handsome young man named Taliaferro Mills.

He was, as I said, quite handsome, but even more compelling was the sense I felt that Tally — as he requested I call him — was different from other boys.

We immediately and effortlessly engaged in a discussion about a variety of subjects: books, education, religion, politics, slavery, and the war. One thing I liked about Tally right off is that he was not ashamed, as are most boys, to admit how much he enjoyed reading.

Tally appeared eager to hear my opinions, which I considered quite flattering. It is not that I consider myself brilliant, but I know that my views are just as profound as the ones boys put forth as if they are in private possession of the wisdom of the ages.

More than anyone else I ever met, Tally

seemed to challenge me with his seriousness. At first I found this quite disarming, causing me to blush, I fear. I also found it, however, quite refreshing.

He also has a way of looking sad, which made me care for him even more.

He asked if I would like some night air and perhaps a glass of punch, and I readily agreed to both. We made our way to the portico, which was lit by a full moon. It seemed to me that night that the moon had never shone as brightly.

Later that evening, when we finally bid everyone good night, Cousin Rachel and I retired to her room. She sleeps in a beautiful four-poster bed and still keeps the steps beside it that she used as a little girl to get in and out.

I learned from her that Tally's parents were tragically killed two years ago in a fire while he was away at school. They have joined the ranks of the blessed. Perhaps this accounts for his serious manner.

She chided me for flirting with him, pointing

out that I hardly spent a minute with anyone else during the entire evening.

I replied that I simply preferred, having found someone to my liking, to spend time with him, rather than have one silly conversation after another.

Cousin Rachel said that she herself preferred having one silly conversation after another — which caused us both to laugh uproariously until we embraced, tears of mirth running down our cheeks, both of us, I fear, feeling the effects of the wonderful punch.

During the long journey home all I could talk about was Tally. Mother, as she often does, warned me not to judge people at first sight. I must confess that she is right; I do tend to do that, but I trust my instincts and I do not think that will ever change.

Looking back now on meeting Tally, I can see that he was disturbed by the war and concerned about doing what was honorable.

At the time I did not understand all that was

happening to us and I am not certain that I do now. Perhaps I could have convinced him that he need not have gone off to fight. I am not sure, however, that that would have been the proper thing to do.

The next week he left Richmond to join General Lee's Army of Northern Virginia, which I learned about later when he wrote me this letter:

Dear Emma,

I felt it my duty to personally acknowledge my debt of gratitude toward you for helping me make what, for me, was a grave and difficult decision.

Your frank comments on the subject of this war, which is surely a plague on our land, helped me formulate my own often complicated views of my responsibilities as a citizen of the South.

By the time you receive this letter I will have joined my Confederate comrades, who are fighting to remove the Yankee invaders from our land.

May I humbly and earnestly request that I might be allowed to write you from time to time,

if my letters can find their way, and that perhaps
you might do me the honor of a reply, if time
permits. My warmest regard to your father and
mother.

> *Sincerely,*
> *Taliaferro Mills*

Lord knows when he will return — when all our gallant boys will return.

She has called upon me to take her place

Friday, January 22, 1864

Mother is not feeling well due to a fever, and she remains in bed. I pray the Lord will provide.

Iris helps me tend to her throughout the day—she is quite devoted. I sat up with Iris for the past two nights while Mother slept peacefully. Iris urged me to go to bed and get some rest, but I am more comfortable being with her and Mother and I think I do doze from time to time on the sofa.

Mother's night table is now cluttered with bottles of medicine and various liquids, including quinine, which Doctor Harris says will help reduce her fever.

Sunday, January 24, 1864

This morning Mother was well enough to sit up in the large chair in the corner of the room by the big bay window.

I brushed her hair, as I know she likes to look presentable.

She was quite grateful.

Mother has asked me to see to it that the weekly classes with the Negro children continue as before her illness. Mother has always seen to the education of her little scholars. I know she feels badly that she is unable to leave her bed chamber and is quite distressed that she cannot carry on her duties as before, but Doctor Harris insists she rest.

I am proud that she has called upon me to take her place.

I tried my best with them but, I must say, it is a trial. They are more interested in playing than hearing stories from the Bible and it is quite tedious reading to them while they fidget about.

Iris helps as we begin class at ten each Wednesday morning, although few of the children arrive on time. Iris's darling daughter, Dinah, is a shining exception, arriving promptly and eager to begin.

I have resolved to do my utmost to ease Mother's mind while she recuperates.

I pray each night that Mother's fever will be gone.

Monday, February 1, 1864

I have been unable to write for the past week. Mother's illness has caused me to sink into a melancholy state. Doctor Harris says she needs time to regain her health and that nothing will help more than rest and quiet. He reassures us that merciful are the ways of the Lord.

Wednesday, February 3, 1864

Aunt Caroline, Cousin Rachel, and Baby Elizabeth have come from Richmond to stay with us. We had to put up the crib for the baby, who stays in Father's room.

Aunt Caroline says they have come because of the state of affairs in Richmond, but I think they have come because of Mother's condition. I keep these thoughts to myself, however, not even mentioning them to Cousin Rachel.

Baby Elizabeth seems to be the only one who is truly happy these days. I gave her a warm bath this morning, which she seemed to enjoy immensely. Afterward she played with the doll I made her for Christmas, but never sent. Tending to the baby helped take my mind briefly from my concern for Mother.

Saturday, February 6, 1864

I feel so very helpless. Thank the Lord for Aunt Caroline and Cousin Rachel. I do not know what I would have done without them. Their presence is such a comfort.

When will this cruel war be over?

Sunday, February 7, 1864

I am finding it difficult to obtain ink. We no longer have any coffee or salt, and Aunt Caroline says that everything is high priced these days.

Tuesday, February 9, 1864

We hear that more Negroes have gone off to join the Yankees. God bless our Negroes, who remain loyal.

When will this cruel war be over?

Sunday, February 14, 1864

Cousin Rachel is quite disturbed that she has not received any Valentine's Day cards. She said that previously she received over a dozen — which was more than anyone in her school.

Monday, February 15, 1864

Mother has improved somewhat — which is a great relief to me — although she has lost weight and still looks quite tired. She is so weak she cannot hold a book in her hands. It is quite distressing to see her in this state. I know how much Mother dislikes being ill and unable to perform her duties. It would be a great comfort to her if Father were here.

I am reading to her each morning and she naps in the early afternoon.

Tuesday, February 16, 1864

There are many reports of smallpox in the area.

Friday, February 19, 1864

Mother is feeling better today. How merciful are the ways of the Lord. She says she enjoys my reading aloud to her so much that it is the first thing she thinks of when she awakes each morning.

We are reading *Wuthering Heights*, which Mother listens to with rapt attention, sometimes requesting I reread a particular passage. This morning she asked to hear Catherine's speech to Isabella concerning her infatuation with Heathcliff.

As I have said, I find Heathcliff a loathsome

creature and fail to understand what attraction he holds for these two women.

Saturday, February 20, 1864

Aunt Caroline has been a dear help to Mother in managing the servants.

The household continues as before, thanks to her efforts. Mother, thank the Lord, has been well enough to spend some time in the morning with Dolphy, going over the clothes that need mending so badly. It is impossible to get new ones and we are fortunate that Dolphy is such a wonderful seamstress.

Iris sees to it that all the rooms are in order, everything dusted and swept and the beds made, although we are, of course, expecting no one. Father would have wanted it that way, she says.

I asked Cousin Rachel if she wanted to pull the breast bone of the guinea hen we had for dinner so we could see who would marry first. She said she would prefer not, as she thought it a silly thing to do and that she considered marriage just as silly.

I must confess, I was startled by this. Cousin Rachel is rather high bred and seems to be putting on airs quite a bit of the time. Perhaps it is because she is older than me — although only by three years.

Sunday, February 21, 1864

The baby is cutting a tooth and Aunt Caroline is awake most of the night tending to her. I help when I can.

Monday, February 22, 1864

Colonel James has been killed, although there was no notice of it in the papers. Mrs. James's oldest son was killed the first year of the war and now she is a widow with three young children to care for.

Tuesday, February 23, 1864

Mother remained in bed all day.

Saturday, February 27, 1864

Aunt Caroline has had great difficulty all week due to problems with her teeth. Six had to be extracted and the long and painful operation, without the benefit of gas, has left her with a grave shock to her system. This coupled with her exhaustion due to the baby has caused Aunt Caroline to look wan and tired.

I simply want Tally to return safely

Thursday, March 3, 1864

O glorious day—a letter from Tally. The letter was dated Christmas Day, and he seemed disconsolate.

He says the weather is quite cold and when the rain and sleet fall icicles hang from their hats and clothes. Many of the men are badly frostbitten, and some have froze to death along the roadside. He has seen enough of the glory of war, and he marvels at the ability of those around him to get used to the deprivations they are forced to endure.

I hope it is not childish to think of my own feelings when the war is being waged about such grave issues—but I cannot help that I simply want Tally to return safely.

He reports that they have been expecting an engagement for the past two weeks but that, thus far, it has not come—which is just as well with him. They are in winter quarters and the men are quite restive. One soldier on lookout duty was found asleep at his post. He was, Tally says, brought up before a court-martial but his life was spared.

Everyone believes the Yankees are just in front of them and the battle is looming. He says that the fighting has resulted in great slaughter on both sides and that he has lost many friends. He has seen quite enough of a soldier's life. The Yankee artillery is so fearsome — felling every upright thing — that one of his comrades was killed by a shattered tree limb.

There has been little to eat and what they do have — mostly cornmeal, crackers, and bacon — is not enough. They are forced to catch squirrels and rabbits and birds, which they roast at night on sticks since they have few utensils with which to cook. Many of the men are suffering from dysentery and malaria but Tally only has blistered feet.

Even more than good food, he craves sleep. They are constantly kept in a weary state — at night they sleep on the hard ground.

He says it is difficult to remain and fight knowing that those back home are suffering every day. But he feels this is his duty and cannot forsake it. Some men are so desperate to return to their homes that they have taken extraordinary measures. He observed one man who purposely shot off his finger in order to obtain a furlough. Sometimes it is as if he is in a dream and he wonders what it will be like when he wakes. Many of the men are growing sick of the war and are deserting. He says a battlefield is the saddest sight he has ever seen.

Writing paper is quite scarce, and he is writing in between the lines so he can say as much as possible. It is indeed difficult to read. My letters are a great comfort to him and he hopes I will not tire of writing.

He has sent me a ring which I must confess was quite a surprise, although a pleasant one. He says he will be home soon — although I am afraid to believe that that is true. I fear that my faith is not that strong. The ring is too small and I have placed it on a silver chain which I wear around my neck, but only when I am in my room alone, as I fear it would upset Mother — thinking Tally too forward and too old for me — as if eighteen were that much older than almost fifteen. I know we have only met once, and then briefly, but I know my heart.

The ring is too dear to me to just place it in a drawer

Saturday, March 5, 1864

The Broyles brothers have both returned home due to wounds received fighting Yankees at Deep Creek.

We have grown accustomed to having no men around

Monday, March 7, 1864

The war has been going on far longer than anyone thought, so long that I fear we have become accustomed to it. We have grown accustomed to having no men around, accustomed to things we had taken for granted — coffee, ink, flour for baking — all becoming precious, and accustomed to all the gaiety having vanished from our lives. We seem to have lost all hope, as if this is the way it will be forever.

Thursday, March 10, 1864

Another letter from Father today. It was difficult for Aunt Caroline to read it. She said she did not think it wise to show the letter to Mother, who has not been well lately and has once again been confined to bed by Doctor Harris.

Father remains confident that our cause will

triumph in the end. He says the Abolitionists may rave as much as they like but the fact is that the Negro race is inferior to the white race and must remain so. He says the Negroes have thrived in the South due to our ever-watchful eyes and are better off with us than with the Yankees.

He is proud to hear that our Negroes have remained loyal and that their behavior proves his argument, for if slavery were as bad as Northerners would have us believe then surely all the Negroes in the South would have abandoned the plantations and gone north by now.

Sadly, he informs us that Jack Fellers was severely wounded and, although the surgeon said there was no danger — which at least allowed him to have a peaceful night's sleep — he was beyond all human help by morning. Father requested that we tell the grievous news to the Fellers family. Father says that the suffering his brave and noble troops have had to endure will prove justified in the end, for their cause is a righteous one. To keep up their spirits, his men recently engaged in a fierce snowball battle. He urges us to pray to God so He will not forsake us during these dark and bloody days. Father has the utmost faith in General Lee, whose dignified presence is a solace to all around him and fills the men with pride, knowing that they are guided by his calm hand. Father has not been wounded and believes God has kept him in the hollow of His hand.

I do not know if Father is aware of Mother's condition. Each day she seems worse than the one past, and I fear it is becoming too much for me to bear.

Father wonders why we don't write him, which is curious because we have. I cannot help but think that our letters are not getting to their proper destination. The mail — like everything else — seems to be suffering lately.

Sunday, March 20, 1864

Cousin Martha's daughter Bettie has the measles. The whole family fears they may get it also.

There is little to say that is of any real help

Monday, March 21, 1864

We visited Mrs. Fellers today. Their home is under-standably filled with sadness. They were married last year, just previous to Mr. Fellers's leaving. Mrs. Fellers does not even have any children to remember him by. This is what this terrible war has brought to our land.

Needless to say she was beside herself with grief. Aunt Caroline did her best to console her but, as we all know, there is little to say that is of any real help.

Wednesday, March, 23, 1864

Mother is still feeling poorly.

Thursday, March 24, 1864

Cousin Rachel has been quite a trial since she arrived. For some time I thought she was cross with me — but now I know that that is not so. Like all of us she is shaken because her world has been pulled out from under her. I think her father's death affected her greatly, although she says nothing about it directly.

We talked in my room until late in the evening, drinking tea sweetened with brown sugar, which helps relieve some of our anxiety.

She is greatly disturbed that she has had to leave her school. Knowing that she may never return distresses her. The school was closed due to the war. Cousin Rachel, however, explained to me that she had to return home even before that, having become ill with what the doctors say is a weak stomach.

She went on about the school quite at length. It is apparent that she liked it a great deal.

Cousin Rachel lived with four other girls in a large room. She took drawing classes, French, piano, flute, and musical composition, in addition to other studies. Her French teacher was Mademoiselle Vaucher, who was from France.

In the evenings there was a two-hour study

period, during which time Cousin Rachel said she and her roommates studied little, preferring to debate the merits of marriage and gossip about the cadets at the nearby military academy. Precisely at ten o'clock the lights were turned out — a practice that was strictly enforced by proctors patrolling the halls.

She misses the theater parties, the fancy balls, the Friday evening musical soirees, and eating with her friends in the school dining room — although she was quick to point out that the school's fare compared quite unfavorably to what she was accustomed to at home.

From time to time they had Sunday dinner at Susan Anne Taylor's home, where they feasted on oysters, turkey, fish, venison, pound cake, strawberries, and marmalade. Susan Anne was one of Cousin Rachel's roommates and her closest friend. I gather that she misses her company, and I am afraid I cannot provide Cousin Rachel with that kind of companionship, try as I might.

Although I have always appreciated the fact

that Mother sees to my education, I have, none-theless, been curious about what it is like going away to school, as Cousin Rachel did, and I quite enjoyed listening to her.

She admitted that she has been behaving sourly.

Cousin Rachel has a great many opinions that she holds quite strongly. She says she will never be governed by what others think, and she will do what her conscience dictates.

She thinks that boys hide their real feelings and true characters and are not to be trusted, and that many girls foolishly marry boys who are unworthy, something she says she has no intention of doing. She maintains that girls are in every way superior to boys, and she believes that married life is infinitely taxing and she will never embark on that course.

It would be foolish, she says, to agree to marry with the war raging over our land. You might, she points out, be a widow before long.

I am not sure I agree with all of this. Cousin Rachel seems so sure of her views; perhaps when

I am her age I will come to agree with her, but for now I am afraid I do not.

Saturday, March 26, 1864

I no longer read aloud to Mother, as she cannot stay awake for long. I wish Father were here — I would not be so afraid if he were. Our only hope is in the Lord, though He seems far off.

Wednesday, March 30, 1864

The snow is almost gone. I am worried about Mother. Doctor Harris has been here twice this week.

I am beside myself with fear

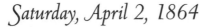

Saturday, April 2, 1864

Our troops passed near here today. They looked quite destitute. Many of them had no shoes. For one brief moment I thought I saw Tally among them. But it was only a boy, a young boy. Like Tally he was taller than the others, and he had the same curly brown hair and piercing, sad blue eyes. I was relieved that it was not him, for the boy looked quite forlorn.

Tuesday, April 12, 1864

I have not written for the last two weeks because of Mother's condition. I am beside myself with fear for her and what will become of us.

Doctor Harris is, I am sure, doing his best, but Mother looks more and more tired every day. Doctor Harris said he would be encouraged if Mother would only show a little craving for food, but she hardly takes a nibble, just some tea from time to time. It is more than I can bear to gaze upon her pale countenance. She understands everything and appreciates all we do for her, but somehow it is not enough.

My heart is desolate

Monday, April 18, 1864

Mother died today.

Thursday, April 28, 1864

I have tried not to indulge myself in the dubious luxury of grief — but Mother's leaving has cast a gloomy shroud about the house. It is the saddest event that has yet occurred in my young life. I have tried to behave as Mother would have wanted me to — and, indeed, as she so earnestly requested of me when we last spoke.

I cannot help but remember, with great longing, those glorious days before this horrible war descended upon us and ruined everything. Everything. I cannot help but yearn for a return to that time. Perhaps I will wake one morning and Mother will be busily organizing the servants, going over the chores with Iris, the cooking with Denise, the sewing with Dolphy. O how calmly I write about it.

Mother seemed to spend more and more time confined to bed these past few weeks. That night, Mother was sleeping soundly and I must have dozed off on the sofa, although I was resolved to stay awake. But the next thing I knew someone was gently shaking me and softly calling my name, "Miss Emma, Miss Emma," but the voice seemed far away, like someone calling through a mist, like on the moors in *Wuthering Heights*.

I was afraid to open my eyes, and hoped that the calling would go away and the shaking would stop. But whoever was calling would not stop and the shaking persisted. I willed my eyes to open and perceived Iris, her black face glistening with the tracks of her tears saying, "Miss Emma, your Mother wishes to see you."

I still did not know whether or not I was dreaming. I told Iris that I had to comb my hair first, but Iris said that that would wait, and helped me rise and led me to Mother's bedside.

The room was gray, the morning sun just beginning to cast its light. I placed my hand on Mother's brow, which felt moist, and reached for a cloth that was kept on the night table. Tenderly I wiped the sweat from her forehead and waited for her eyes to open.

Mother looked so serene and regal lying there. A light seemed to frame her beautiful face, and I could see that the pain and suffering were no longer etched there.

It seemed like quite some time before Mother opened her eyes. When she did I could see that her dark brown eyes were telling me to prepare myself. She pulled me near, which must have taken all her strength. "Dearest child," she said, "I fear my health is failing me, and I will not be able to care for you as before." Tears filled her eyes, but none fell. "Be sure to help Aunt Caroline," she continued, her voice almost a whisper, "and spend as little time as possible on tears, for tears will do us all no good. We must trust in the Lord's blessing."

She asked me if I understood and I said that

I had, although I must confess that I honestly do not understand.

Suddenly, my body felt chilled to the bone. All I could think about was how well Mother had borne up during her illness and that I now must do the same.

It was only then that I realized Aunt Caroline was there. She put her arm around me and led me to my room, where I clutched the daguerreotype of Mother that I always kept next to my bed and sobbed till somehow I must have fallen asleep.

I was unable to attend Mother's burial in the family graveyard. When I saw the men coming to take her away, my heart stopped beating and I turned from the window and sobbed in my bed, unable to rise. I could not bear it.

Aunt Caroline came to my room later and said I should not be concerned about not attending Mother's burial. She said she would do all she could to give me the love and care she knew I would dearly miss and that, although she knew no one could ever replace Mother, she would do her best to help.

I have tried as best I can to obey Mother's last wish, although, I must confess, I have spent a great deal of time in my room. My heart is desolate.

Although I was ashamed of my selfish behavior, I could not help it. My room provided me with the solitude I needed — at least for the time — and I spent countless hours sitting in my window, watching the Negroes come and go.

Friday, April 29, 1864

Aunt Caroline reminds me so much of Mother. Like Mother, she seems resolved to these times and, like Mother, she has an unshakable faith in the Lord. She talks to Cousin Rachel and me about trusting the Lord, but I am not sure I can have the kind of faith that she and Mother have.

Baby Elizabeth is quite pretty, just like her mother. The same sparkling blue eyes. Aunt Caroline allowed me to put her to sleep for the first time. I rocked her and sang "Three Little Kittens" and "Hush-a-Bye, Baby."

Sunday, May 8, 1864

After breakfast we took the carriage into town and attended church for the first time in quite a while. Aunt Caroline said that it was the most wonderful sermon, but I heard little of it, my mind filled with thoughts of Mother. Mrs. Broyles, Mr. and Mrs. Garlington, Cousin Martha, and Mrs. Fellers expressed their greatest sympathy.

Tuesday, May 10, 1864

We received word of the death of Lieutenant Walker.

I must write tonight

Wednesday, May 11, 1864

I took a walk in the garden, which helped soothe me. In the distance the apple orchard was a radiant field of large, white, billowing balls.

How I loved to idle away the hours, walking the garden paths, while Mother tended to her plants, weeding, hoeing, and pruning them with great care and patience, often assisted by Amos, who seemed to care for them almost as much as she did.

Being there reminds me of how much pride Mother took in her garden, especially the rose garden, which was her special joy. It was known throughout Gordonsville, and Mother took great delight in showing guests around it.

I remember one particular day last spring, when Mother and I left the garden, our arms filled with pink and red roses, some of which I took up to my room to dry and some of which Mother gave to Iris, who made them into rosewater.

A rose garden, Mother liked to say, helped remind us that nothing beautiful in life comes without thorns.

I cherished the time I spent in the garden with Mother, and I try to care for the flowers even more now that she is no longer here to tend to them.

Thursday, May 12, 1864

I received a letter from Father today.

My dearest daughter:

I am today in possession of a letter from your Aunt Caroline providing me with the sad intelligence that your precious mother is no longer in this world.

I am certain that her unexpected and lamentable departure has caused you to suffer great sorrow. Words of consolation often fail at times like these. I can only say that it is a great comfort to me to know that your dear, loving mother will abide in heaven, where she will joyously join her precious son in the hollow of His hand. Merciful are the ways of the Lord.

I urge you to take some consolation in that knowledge. Aunt Caroline has kept me informed of your circumstances, which I know are quite difficult to bear. Such is the way throughout much of our hallowed land.

These circumstances have been visited upon us by the Abolitionists from the North, who have invaded our land and forced us to respond with all the means at our command. Please take refuge in knowing, as I do, that our proud Confederacy is watched over by a kind providence and that there will come a time when we will surely return to the life we knew and cherished before the Abolitionists chose this blasphemous and brutal course of action.

It gives me great pain to know that I cannot be with you at this time. I know you must be grieving sorely, feeling the severity of your loss. Although I would dearly like to return home to give you some comfort, my duty is here, with my men.

Trust in the Lord, as I do.

Your Father

64

Wednesday, May 18, 1864

A week has almost passed since I last wrote in my diary.

The Negroes seem confused, and I feel it is no wonder. Last night I heard them singing their beautiful songs.

Thursday, May 19, 1864

Cousin Rachel does love to talk. We talked all day about marriage, which appears to be Cousin Rachel's favorite topic. She went on at length about how men are full of deception, and that young girls must take care to protect themselves. Cousin Rachel says it is better if we are cautious in affairs of the heart. I told her I agreed — at least I nodded quite frequently — but in my heart, especially when I think of Tally, I am not quite sure I share her feelings. I look forward to, some day, being married, for I consider that the natural course of life.

Tuesday, May 24, 1864

Cousin Rachel and I talked in my room again this evening.

Saturday, May 28, 1864

Aunt Caroline and I spent the better part of the day preparing bandages that are to be brought to the church. Our sick and wounded soldiers are being cared for there.

I talked to Aunt Caroline for the first time about how frightened I was this past winter while Mother was confined to bed — how diligently I prayed each night that Mother would get well and how disturbed I was that she remained pale, thin, and weak. And how I imagine her still walking about the house, seeing that everything was proceeding smoothly, just the way she always did.

Aunt Caroline has been patient and loving and no one could ask for more. But no one can ever replace Mother. I miss her terribly. O wicked day. Sometimes I feel as if I will be overwhelmed by sadness. But this is no time for tears, as Mother said.

Sunday, May 29, 1864

There is talk of a terrific battle just east of here — near Spotsylvania Courthouse. Terrible casualties are feared on both sides.

Monday, May 30, 1864

I must write tonight. I confess that I do not feel up to the task. I wonder if every Monday will be blue, for that is the day that Mother bid us good-bye forever.

Friday, June 3, 1864

No one dresses prettily anymore. I thought about this because I was considering what to wear this morning and saw my white cambric dress, the one with the roses on it, the one I wore when I met Tally.

Monday, June 6, 1864

Reports are that there has been a ferocious battle at Cold Harbor, near Richmond. Although it is thought that the cost was great, General Lee's army has, it is believed, emerged victorious.

Despite the heat I have tried to tend to the garden.

Tuesday, June 7, 1864

Cousin Rachel has a very bad sore throat — perhaps if she talked less her throat would not be under such strain. It is no wonder she has a raging fever. Doctor Harris says there is nothing to be concerned about, but of course Doctor Harris also counseled that Mother would recover with the proper care and rest. Cousin Rachel is miserable, and Aunt Caroline is in and out of her room with tea and honey.

I gave Baby Elizabeth her bath again this evening.

Thursday, June 9, 1864

Mr. and Mrs. Garlington paid a visit. He is very grave, while she says little. They talked in the parlor all morning in hushed tones. It scares me.

Tuesday, June 14, 1864

Cousin Rachel lectured me again today about boys. When I brought her breakfast she told me it was important not to be taken in by them, because they are fickle. Cousin Rachel seems old beyond her years, and in some ways bitter.

All the boys are gone now

Thursday, June 16, 1864

A letter from Father.

Aunt Caroline read the letter aloud in the parlor. In attendance were Mr. and Mrs. Garlington, Doctor Harris, and Mrs. Broyles, with Lily and Lucy. Cousin Rachel barely said a word to them, which made me quite unhappy. Cousin Rachel can be quite discourteous at times. They were all very eager for any news about the fighting. Mrs. Broyles is quite concerned about the condition of her sons.

Father says he wishes he could be with us but he does not think that will happen soon. He writes about how important it is to have faith in our just cause and how important it is not to let the Abolitionists subjugate us and take away our country. He says he is on a glorious mission and he will not rest until the vandals are driven from our soil. His spirits are good, for he believes the Lord is with us.

He said it was his painful duty to inform us of the death of Captain Rawlings. They were crossing a river and his horse threw him and, evidently, Mr. Rawlings could not swim. Before Father could offer any assistance, Captain Rawlings had drowned. They did all they could to bring him back to life but it was to no avail. He requested that Aunt Caroline break the news to Mrs. Rawlings and the children. Poor Mrs. Rawlings. I am sure she has only just recovered from the death of her baby girl. The baby was so ill following her premature arrival that Mrs. Rawlings decided not to have the dear, sweet child christened. The baby survived until the third week in February and then was laid in her tiny coffin. Mrs. Rawlings was nearly demented with grief.

Father does not sound as hopeful as he once did, despite his brave words. It seems to me that things have changed. No longer do we turn out waving handkerchiefs and flags, dressed in our finery to bid our brave boys good-bye. All the boys are gone now.

Friday, June 24, 1864

All talk is about Yankees.

There is no more salt, and Dolphy says she hardly has enough needles for sewing. Aunt Caroline says that a barrel of flour costs $70.

Saturday, June 25, 1864

I slept very late this morning and had breakfast in my room. At times the sadness about Mother overwhelms me.

The Broyles brothers continue to suffer terribly from the wounds they received in battle. Tom lost both legs, which were shattered by balls from Yankee rifles and had to be amputated immediately, without the benefit of chloroform or morphine. Robert's wounds are less severe. Needless to say, Mrs. Broyles is quite beside herself.

Lily and Lucy tend to their brothers as best they can.

O what a strange war it is

Tuesday, June 28, 1864

I received a letter from Tally today—dear Tally. I miss him terribly.

He complains that the war is going badly and the men are discouraged and tired of seeing things so unspeakable that he can not commit them to paper. He believes our efforts are futile and curses the politicians who got us into this war—politicians who stay home while his comrades are falling in gruesome sacrifice.

He says it rained most of last week and they had no tents. All around them is mud, mud, mud.

They are hungry and many of the boys are returning home to protect their families. He will continue to fight because he does not want to abandon his comrades.

Tally told about coming upon some Yankees at a place where they were separated only by a creek. They were so close they could holler to each other, and one of the Yankees proposed that they put down their arms and meet midway. They agreed to bargain, and built a raft and met in the middle of the creek, where they traded for canteens, coffee, and tobacco. Tally misses coffee more than anything else, besides sleep.

O what a strange war it is.

Tally asks that we send him clothing — his are in rags. He could use new boots, a hat, some undershirts, and socks. I have not told him about Mother, so he still sends his greetings to her. He signs his letter affectionately yours. I miss him terribly.

Saturday, July 2, 1864

Cousin Rachel was injured yesterday riding Tempest, who, it appears, was frightened by something and threw her ten feet in the air. She fell upon her left side and was knocked insensible. Amos found her and she is now in bed, unable to move. Doctor Harris examined her and she does not have a fracture, which is a relief to us all.

In the morning I brought Cousin Rachel

buttermilk and biscuits for breakfast. She did not drink the buttermilk, but did eat one of the biscuits. For lunch I brought ham, green apples, and cheese, although I fear that is the last of the ham.

I asked her if she would like me to stay so we could have a chat and she said she did. I continued to knit the socks and gloves I am going to send Tally.

I am going to bring Cousin Rachel her breakfast each morning and try to cause her to be less gloomy.

She had barely recovered from her sore throat and probably should not have been out riding. Besides, there is too much danger about.

Those eyes haunted me

Monday, July 4, 1864

To celebrate — hardly the word — Aunt Caroline and I brought as much food as we could spare — some apples, nuts, grapes, a bottle of Father's good wine — and roses from Mother's garden to the poor Broyles boys, who have still not recovered from their grievous wounds. You could see that it lifted their hearts, although they looked so wistful and forlorn. Their eyes followed us as we left their house. Those eyes haunted me later, resulting in a restless night.

Aunt Caroline placed a small Confederate flag on the dinner table to mark the day.

Thursday, July 7, 1864

I am trying to be more pleasant in my daily conversations with Cousin Rachel. She can be quite trying at times. Mother always believed it was an art I should practice — not sheer flattery.

That is nonsense. But she said I must pay more attention to pleasing people, conversing about the things they wished to converse about. She told me from time to time that I was too willful and that sometimes I should not express my thoughts so freely.

Friday, July 8, 1864

There is talk of the Negroes leaving. Mr. Garlington said he overheard Nelson telling one of the younger ones which way to go when they ran off to join the Yankees. Nelson is surely one of the more clever Negroes we have ever had. Father believes he requires careful watching.

We have always treated Nelson as one of our family. When he was a little boy Mother nursed him back to health when he was ill with the fever. I am surprised at his ingratitude if indeed Mr. Garlington can be believed. He thinks they have forgotten their place. It is hard for me to judge.

Saturday, July 9, 1864

My watch is broken.

Monday, July 11, 1864

Cousin Martha and Bettie visited today. They have fully recovered from the measles, which plagued the entire family for weeks. Cousin Martha says the Yankees will not rest until they have killed every one of us.

Tuesday, July 12, 1864

Mr. Garlington and his wife visited today. They say the Yankees are different creatures than we are, that they do not worship the same Lord. We are, Mr. Garlington says, like oil and water and will not mix. It is best, he says, we go our separate ways — that is the Lord's will.

Cousin Rachel appears to be recovering from her fall. She is walking about and is able to join Aunt Caroline, Baby Elizabeth, and me for breakfast. The baby is growing each day, and her various utterances are sounding more like words. Today is her first birthday. We celebrated by singing and playing the piano in the parlor.

I pray that the Yankees will soon leave our land

Friday, July 15, 1864

Aunt Caroline, Cousin Rachel, and I have been working all day cutting and sewing shirts and making bandages for our valiant boys. I pray that providence will watch over them. I pray that the Yankees will soon leave our land and allow us to resume our lives.

Wednesday, July 20, 1864

One of the Negroes—a little girl named Cinda— has been taken violently ill with scarlet fever.

Saturday, July 23, 1864

Cinda died today.

The moonlight last night reminded me of Tally, the night we met at Aunt Caroline's.

Sunday, July 24, 1864

The weather is quite warm today.

Monday, July 25, 1864

Aunt Caroline, Mrs. Broyles, and Mr. Garlington and his wife talked in hushed tones in the parlor nearly all day. They do not want Cousin Rachel and me to hear, but we slip in unnoticed when the conversation is especially heated and silently settle upon the sofa under the window. The talk is, of course, about the war. There is disagreement about how it is going. Mr. Garlington is certain that we will emerge victorious, but the others are not so optimistic. They fear our boys are tired to the bone. The talk is all dark and dreadful.

Tuesday, July 26, 1864

One of the Negroes was run over by a wagon. We expect he will recover.

Wednesday, July 27, 1864

Aunt Caroline and I visited the Broyles boys today. Cousin Rachel declined to accompany us.

They are sorely in need of food and are, I fear, doing poorly, especially Tom. It is quite distressing to see those valiant boys lying there in such discomfort.

Tom called out in his delirium that he was going home now, and sat up and began trying to put on his shoes.

The air is filled with restlessness

Thursday, July 28, 1864

Tom Broyles has died. May the Lord protect us.
I try to keep my faith in Him.

Friday, July 29, 1864

Bless our Negroes for they are very faithful.
Everyone is complaining about their Negroes,
although I cannot see much change in ours.
They still appear to me to be cheerful, loyal, and
well behaved. Amos still takes me for rides
and teaches me all the little tricks he knows.
Some of the Negroes are lazy—but, then again,
I think that was always the case with some.
Sometimes I wonder what goes on behind
their masks.

Saturday, July 30, 1864

Cousin Rachel and I were excused after dinner.
The talk in the parlor seemed particularly

heated. The air is filled with restlessness. All we can do is await our fate.

Cousin Rachel talked again, at length, about missing school. She seems quite distressed and talks for hours at a time, and then lapses into silence for days.

Everyone talks as if they were just tables and chairs

Tuesday, August 2, 1864

It is impossible for me to tell if the Negroes understand what is taking place — they come and go as usual, serving dinner while everyone talks as if they were just tables and chairs.

I am not sure Mother would permit this if she were here. Mr. Garlington believes they are wiser than we think — "we" means Aunt Caroline, who seems in constant disagreement with him and Doctor Harris. He thinks they are simply biding their time, waiting for the Yankees to set them free.

Wednesday, August 3, 1864

I spend more and more time tending Mother's garden. I picked some red roses to place on the dinner table.

The house is so quiet. It used to be filled with

visitors. The second- and third-floor guest rooms were nearly always occupied. Now the house is empty and we rattle about.

I sat in my window, well after everyone was asleep, dreaming of days gone by and wondering if we will ever laugh again.

Thursday, August 4, 1864

I am reading *Jane Eyre*, which helps occupy my mind. I am enjoying it more than anything in recent memory. Jane Eyre certainly has a sharp eye. Her descriptions of those around her are precise and unforgiving.

Friday, August 5, 1864

Aunt Caroline — with her soft, sweet, soothing voice; her graceful, caring ways; and her bright blue eyes that seem to peer into your very soul — has been a constant comfort to me these past three and a half months. Like Mother she assures me that the Lord will not forsake us. I try to keep my faith.

I have done my best to help her take Mother's

place and run the house. I owe her much, and I hope I have not disappointed her. At times I am tempted to sink into melancholy, but then I remember Mother's last words — tears will do us all no good — and I fight back those tears and help Aunt Caroline with the tasks at hand.

I continue to imagine Mother once again descending the stairs, greeting Iris, dispatching Denise, sitting with Dolphy, and seeing to it that all the little things are set about in an orderly fashion and making sure that everything is just so.

Aunt Caroline and I are doing the best we can. Our servants have, I think, done their share. Especially Iris.

Of all my students, Dinah is the most attentive. She always arrives promptly, eager to begin her lessons. At times I am able to sit with Dinah later in the week and go over her writing and spelling, which she seems most concerned about and, I must confess, I feel most comfortable teaching.

I think a great deal of Dinah's attitude is due to her mother's persistent urging. I am proud of them both. I know Iris appreciates my efforts and that helps me continue.

At times I imagine Mother's happy face beaming down. How I long for her praise. When Mother was pleased I could feel a warm glow about me.

The newspapers are filled with woeful reports

❧

Saturday, August 6, 1864

So much of what is me comes from Mother. Just reading again reminds me of that. Everyone always knew that the best gift to give Mother was a book. One of my lasting images is of Mother peacefully reading her book in the parlor while Father read his papers or played dominoes with Brother Cole.

Like Mother, I too would read during those long, serene evenings. I hope I am thought of like Mother when I have my own family.

This morning I rose at first light, eager to continue the story of Jane Eyre. I feel so badly for her — she seems so lonely, with little to raise her spirits — yet she bears up so well. I have a growing respect for her perseverance in the face of grave adversity.

However, I am trying not to spend too much

time reading in my room, as I think it worries Aunt Caroline, who has enough to do taking care of Baby Elizabeth and keeping a watchful eye on Cousin Rachel.

Sunday, August 7, 1864

There are nothing but Negroes all around us. All the men, except, of course, Mr Garlington and Doctor Harris, have gone off to war.

Mr. Garlington thinks our Negroes are spoiled, but I think they just have good manners. Maybe it is merely an act and I am being fooled—that is what Cousin Rachel thinks—but I am afraid she always sees the worst in people.

Spent a good portion of the day tending to the horses, who, I fear, have been neglected. Falla's colt is growing quite steadily.

Monday, August 8, 1864

I spent a quiet day reading in my room. Aunt Caroline is in the parlor, and I have not seen Cousin Rachel.

Robert Broyles has disappeared. His mother

thinks he may have headed south, but no one knows.

Tuesday, August 9, 1864

I am not recording all the rumors that are about. The newspapers are filled with woeful reports.

Wednesday, August 10, 1864

Last night I stayed up very late reading *Jane Eyre*; although tired, I could not wait to see what the next chapter would bring. Her life, like my own, seems to become more complicated with every turn in the road.

Spent a quiet day sewing shirts with Dolphy, who delights in my progress with needle and thread.

Another week — not a word from Tally.

Friday, August 12, 1864

After breakfast I fixed my hair. It has been such a long time since I did that — I honestly cannot remember when I have spent that much time before the mirror. I fixed it the way Aunt

Caroline fixes hers. I plaited it down my back and have worn it that way all day.

I am happy my hair is long.

At dusk I went to the garden and gathered some sweet-smelling roses.

As Jane Eyre says, "Even for me life had its gleams of sunshine."

Sunday, August 14, 1864

Aunt Caroline has suggested that she and Cousin Rachel play together. Cousin Rachel has not played her flute since she arrived, although I know she brought it with her.

Cousin Rachel does not seem to be very happy these days, and we no longer talk as frequently as we did, which, I believe, is largely due to her melancholy moods.

She declined Aunt Caroline's invitation and so Aunt Caroline played in the parlor — she prefers that piano to the others in the house — while I read *Jane Eyre*, which I am liking much more than *Wuthering Heights*.

Aunt Caroline plays beautifully, her long,

slender fingers — her pinkie is as long as her ring finger — lightly dancing over the keys, her head bowed in concentration. At times I can hear her humming the tune as she plays.

Monday, August 15, 1864

Cousin Rachel seems to be practicing her flute for the first time. I can hear her in the early evenings, up in her room. She plays quite nicely and I hope she continues, as I believe it will help keep up her spirits.

She has kept much to herself these past few weeks, but yesterday she returned to her former self and is once again speaking from great heights on any number of issues — the war, Negroes, and especially, marriage.

Her health is suffering once again. She was confined to bed due to a weak stomach and a touch of dysentery. Perhaps it was something she ate.

Tuesday, August 16, 1864

Cousin Rachel dropped her scissors today and they stuck in the floor, which she said is a sign that we would be getting a visitor. She says we all should prepare ourselves.

I think Aunt Caroline is quite concerned about her, although she has not said anything to me.

Wednesday, August 17, 1864

Miss Sally Robbins visited today. It has been a long time since we saw her. She is engaged to Lieutenant Charles Jones and is constantly concerned with his well being. It has been weeks since she's heard from him. Sally Robbins is rather staid, and Cousin Rachel was quite put off by her.

After dinner Cousin Rachel went on — quite at length — lecturing Sally Robbins about her views on marriage, most of which, of course, I am quite familiar with.

Cousin Rachel is quite critical of Sally and states that rushing headlong into marriage is a dreadful path to trod. She spoke at length about the evils of submitting to men and said that it was important for young girls like ourselves to enjoy our lives rather than find ourselves bound to a life of toil and trouble. She says that when we—Sally and me, I suppose—are older we will see that when your heart is broken you will not wish to have it so again.

It was quite a trial for everyone to sit through this discourse politely. Aunt Caroline was so disturbed that she excused herself saying that she wanted to see that the baby was sleeping soundly. The baby had a slight cough all day.

Cousin Rachel's speech was particularly vexing, as she and Sally Robbins are the same age. It was also curious because Cousin Rachel appears to be shielding something from her past. I would have asked her to tell me why she seems so troubled, but it appears that the topic still weighs heavily on her soul so I decided to remain silent.

Thursday, August 18, 1864

While I was working in the garden, Cousin Rachel joined me and continued the conversation of last evening as if we had never parted. She confided that she was becoming quite melancholy and believes she has gone into a steep decline. She says that it is only now and again that she is able to regain her composure. It seems this is not the first time this has happened to her, and it is quite a trial for her.

She said that life is a bitter cup from which we are all forced to drink.

Saturday, August 20, 1864

Another week has passed and still not one word from Tally.

Sunday, August 21, 1864

I must confess that at times I simply wish Cousin Rachel would learn to conduct herself in a more appealing fashion. Her behavior with Sally Robbins was quite embarrassing.

Wednesday, August 24, 1864

I spent the evening alone, reading *Jane Eyre* in my room. Her thoughts eerily mirror my own:

It is a very strange sensation to inexperienced youth to feel itself quite alone in the world, cut adrift from every connection, uncertain whether the port to which it is bound can be reached, and prevented by many impediments from returning to that it has quitted. . . .

I will do my best: it is a pity that doing one's best does not always answer.

The war is at our door

Thursday, August 25, 1864

All talk is of Atlanta. The Yankees are rumored to be preparing to invade the city. There is an air here of hopelessness. Many of our friends and neighbors are coming to bid us farewell—perhaps forever.

Sunday, August 28, 1864

Last night I looked out my window and saw men in the trees watching the house. I trembled with fear and felt a chill, despite the heat.

The war is at our door.

Monday, August 29, 1864

The Yankees have invaded the Broyleses' house. When Mrs. Broyles woke, the garden was filled with soldiers, their bayonets glistening in the early morning sunlight. They broke the window, stole food, and within minutes the house was filled with rough men and no officer in attendance.

Then they left just as suddenly as they had come. Mrs. Broyles was too frightened to stay there, and took Lily and Lucy and began the journey to our house. She was fortunate enough, when they were three miles away, to see Amos, who gave them a ride in his cart. Amos was good enough to provide umbrellas so they did not suffer from the intense heat.

Mrs. Broyles says she was so startled by the intrusion that she imagines any noise now to be a recurrence, and she cannot stop her heart from palpitating so fearfully that it frightens her. She said one of the Yankees told her that they were not going to let Rebels sleep comfortably in their homes while their own wounded and sick men suffered.

All of the Negroes welcomed the Yankees with open arms. The Negroes told the Yankees about the bloodhound Mr. Broyles used to track down runaways and then went with them to shoot him. The Negroes whooped and hollered in their quarters when they heard the shots and the dog's pitiful howls.

Tuesday, August 30, 1864

As I read late into the night, once again Jane Eyre uncannily has put my feelings into words I possess not the wisdom to conjure:

> I was in my own room as usual — just myself, without obvious change . . . where was the Jane Eyre of yesterday? Where was her life? Where were her prospects?

This is all some horrible dream

❦

Thursday, September 1, 1864

Early this morning we learned that the Broyleses' house was taken over by Yankees. A Yankee officer came by and advised us that his troops would not injure anyone but that the house was required for a hospital to tend to his wounded men.

We are all quite startled by this turn of events, but Aunt Caroline has cautioned that we must remain calm. I am doing my utmost to live up to her expectations, although part of me yearns to believe that this is all some horrible dream from which I will soon awake.

Saturday, September 3, 1864

Today, at dawn, a Yankee soldier came to our house and asked me if I would tell him where our troops are. I refused—although, of course, I have no information as to their whereabouts. The soldier said he was tired of the war and wished to go home, and if I would tell him where they could be found, it would help him make his escape. He said he had been willing to fight to save the Union but that now the war was being fought by Abolitionists who want to free the slaves — he wished to fight no more.

I said I knew nothing that could help him, and the man rode off. He seemed quite agitated, and Cousin Rachel says he was drunk. We were all quite shaken by the ordeal. Our troops are nowhere to be seen. It is thought that they have been forced to withdraw in the face of Yankee advances.

When we sat down to breakfast the house was surrounded by Yankees, who threatened to destroy everything if food was not given to them. Cousin Rachel, quite beside herself, ran to lock the front and back doors but they broke down the library door and smashed windows and entered the kitchen and the pantry and carried off all the food they could find.

Monday, September 5, 1864

Everyone is shocked by what is happening to us, but there is little we can do about it.

There are reports that Atlanta is being evacuated and the Yankees are about to capture the city. It is, however, impossible to be certain of anything.

Tuesday, September 6, 1864

One of Mrs. Jane Allen's Negroes ran off with her diamond ring and other jewelry. Mrs. Allen was distraught because the ring belonged to her husband's mother. Mr. Allen was killed earlier this year. She reported the theft to one of the Yankee officers, but he said nothing could be done about it.

Nothing seems safe anymore

Friday, September 9, 1864

I have not written for three days because there has been no time and only bad news to report. Wednesday a Yankee officer presented himself to Aunt Caroline and informed her that our house was to be handed over immediately to him so that it could be turned into a headquarters for the Federal troops in the area. We were to move all our belongings into the third-floor guest rooms or, if we preferred, he would furnish wagons that would carry us wherever we liked.

Aunt Caroline asked him just where he suggested we go. He said he could not help her with that but he was willing to provide conveyances that would carry us, our household articles, and personal possessions.

Aunt Caroline told him we would prefer to stay, and he said he would be returning by midday and to please make sure that everything was attended to. I was so proud of Aunt Caroline. Cousin Rachel burst into tears and ran to her room and locked the door. Mrs. Broyles was not much use either. She simply sat in the kitchen and wept.

Aunt Caroline and I had no other choice but to begin moving everything into the third-floor bedrooms.

Iris called Nelson and Amos and somehow they collected most of what had to be moved. Nelson had to break down Cousin Rachel's door so we could move her things. Cousin Rachel and I are in one room, Aunt Caroline and the baby in another, and the Broyles family in a third.

At midday, while the Yankees were elsewhere, we began hiding the silver and Mother's jewelry. Everything was hidden in the garret. We hope they will be safe — although nothing seems safe anymore.

We had to step around Cousin Rachel, who appears quite beside herself and was sitting on the stairs sobbing uncontrollably because she had been deprived of her room.

Monday, September 12, 1864

The news is bad all over. Mrs. Cornelia Finch's house has been set aflame. The Yankees came shortly after breakfast and informed Mrs. Finch that she should remove everything from the house — which she did — although it was quite a chore since she has five small children and all her Negroes have run off. There was no one to help her except her invalid brother, who was at least able to hold the baby.

While they were leaving, the Yankees were pouring liquid all over the house, and as they drove away they turned to see the house go up in flames. Amos reports that the house has been burned to the ground.

Tuesday, September 13, 1864

Finishing *Jane Eyre* has left me breathless and thirsting for more.

Her story relieved me of so many of my current concerns — if only for a brief time. She too seemed to exist in the eye of a storm.

I have developed the highest regard for her

character: her steadfastness to principle; her concern for others less fortunate than herself—this despite her own numerous misfortunes; her integrity, even in the face of dire consequences.

I hope someday to be able to emulate these character traits.

I am trying not to feel blue

⚜

Wednesday, September 14, 1864

Mrs. Broyles is refusing to eat and is not looking well. She remains in her room, with Lucy, who seems afraid to leave her side. Fortunately, Lily has proved to be a great help. She has grown quite attached to the baby and helps me tend to her, which is something I have done with more frequency in order to help Aunt Caroline. I do enjoy playing with Baby Elizabeth, who grows more responsive to me with each day. I have been applying oil dutifully to her hair on a daily basis, in hopes that it will curl, but to no avail.

At night I hold her in my arms and sing "Hush-a-Bye, Baby," which has become her favorite song. She falls asleep in my arms after a few minutes, and I lay her quietly in her crib, as my thoughts turn to Jane Eyre:

I watched the slumber of childhood . . . so passionless, so innocent — and waited for the coming of the day.

Friday, September 16, 1864

Aunt Caroline has decided that the silver and the jewelry will not be safe in the garret. Early this morning, after the Yankees had departed, we took everything and put them in holes we dug in the ground behind the garden where the grass slopes down to the pond.

Saturday, September 17, 1864

My birthday.

Aunt Caroline gave me a shawl she had secretly been knitting and a gold thimble and some pins she said belonged to Mother. Denise was able to somehow find enough flour to bake me a cake, and she put a rose on it, because she knew it would remind me of Mother. And Dinah gave me a card she wrote out all by herself. I shall treasure it forever.

I am trying not to feel blue — although it is quite impossible. It is my first birthday without Mother.

I see little hope

Monday, September 19, 1864

A letter from Father.

He says we should not be discouraged, and assures us that the Yankees are an inferior breed, and that the Lord will watch over us and not allow the wicked Abolitionists to prevail. We are locked in what will be a long, valiant struggle but we must have faith in the Lord.

Father maintains that the Abolitionists would like to destroy our country and see the Negroes set free so they could live just like white people, and he is certain that that is not the Lord's plan. He is sure that setting them free would ruin their lives as well as ours.

They are about to move camp, although they have no orders yet, because there is a big battle looming, and it is believed that the Yankees are quite near. The men are steadfast in their determination.

He complains that he has not received a letter recently and wonders what is the reason.

I dearly hope that where he is, the situation is better than here, for I see little hope for us.

Wednesday, September 21, 1864

Everywhere there is turmoil. The Yankees are roaming the countryside, at times drunk. Mr. Garlington says that a rowdy band of Yankees — not commanded by any officer — is demanding five hundred dollars or they threaten to set the house on fire. Some families have paid only to find, sometimes just hours later, another wild band right behind them, making the same demands. There is little one can do. I must confess we have been spared great travail because of the troops who now make their headquarters here at our house. Colonel Davenport has done his utmost to maintain order and keep the soldiers behaving properly. Of course, daily life now has become quite a chore. Putting together a meal is a problem not only because of the scarcity of food — I cannot even remember the last time we had beef—but we have to scurry about the pantry before the soldiers are awake and fix breakfast by candlelight and then bring everything upstairs to the third floor.

Aunt Caroline and I see to it that the baby and Mrs. Broyles are fed first. Mrs. Broyles is looking quite poorly and continues to spend all day in her room, attended by Lucy.

I wonder if he and Father are fighting the same war

Saturday, September 24, 1864

A letter from Tally.

O how glorious I feel even in the midst of the trials of our daily life. Just to know that he is alive is enough to fill me with hope.

I wonder if he and Father are fighting the same war. He says he is so tired of marching and fighting that at times he just throws himself on the hard ground. He has never been so exhausted in all his life. The flies swarm like bees and are an abomination.

He writes that he has never seen so many dead, wounded, and broken men, that this war is taking a dreadful toll. The wounded suffer terribly and the doctors kill more men than they cure. Some suffer dreadful complications from their wounds, and he watches helplessly while they endure their private tortures only to die in the end. Many of them are thirsty and their throats are parched and cracked, their faces blackened with smoke and powder, and they are hungry all the time. He longs for something good to eat.

He writes that one of his friends was captured during a recent skirmish but escaped two days later, making his way to a nearby stream. He was able to remain underwater as the Yankees fired all around him. Believing, at last, that he must be dead, they left, and he returned to camp wet as a rat and covered with mud.

Tally says he has become hardened to the sight of death — a cornfield where one battle was fought had so many dead bodies that he could have walked over it without stepping on the ground. The Yankees outnumber them and have better rifles, which are treasured when they are captured. During a recent fight the Yankees retreated in such haste that they were unable to bury their dead. He has seen enough of war and hopes never to witness it again.

More and more men are deserting every day. Last week someone in his company was caught and condemned to be executed. Tally was forced to be among those in the firing squad. The wretched man, blindfolded, was marched to the designated place and tied to a stake. Tally does not know if his gun was loaded, as half of the men were given blank charges. The man was trying to return home in order to help his family. The letters they receive from home tell of their families having little to eat. He wonders why we have not written to him, although he says he did receive the clothes we sent.

He is of the opinion that they will have another fight soon.

He has changed, he says, although he hopes he is the same Tally I met before he left and the thought of returning home and seeing me is the only thing that keeps him going. He feels fortunate to have escaped injury or worse, or fallen prey to any of the illnesses that are plaguing his comrades, many of whom are suffering from chronic dysentery or typhoid fever.

He says he does not have the words to express his sorrow upon hearing of Mother's passing, but he knows that, in a way, she is still with us. His words are like balm for my soul, and I am relieved that he has received at least one of my letters. He said he never wished to be back home so much in all his life and he wonders if I am receiving his letters. He has not received a letter from me in a long time.

Sunday, September 25, 1864

Cousin Rachel marched down the stairs this morning and demanded to see Colonel Davenport. After much fuss she was admitted into the library, which now serves as his office. She told him she would be unable to enter the house by the front door if he insists on putting up the Union flag. Colonel Davenport said the flag would stand and that this was now Federal property. Cousin Rachel said she would enter and leave only by the back door in that case. Colonel Davenport said Cousin Rachel could do as she wished and had his soldiers escort her from the library.

Tuesday, September 27, 1864

Mr. Garlington remains optimistic, although Lord knows it is hard for me to understand his belief that the Confederate troops are about to push back the Yankees.

I am glad Mother is not here to see what has happened

Wednesday, September 28, 1864

I visited the family graveyard today. I am glad Mother is not here to see what has happened. Sometimes I am thrown into a state of melancholy when I think about her and the days that seem gone forever. Mother, reading aloud to me while the fire warmed us. I especially remember the first autumn fires — how brightly they burned. I doubt if they will ever burn quite so brightly again.

Friday, September 30, 1864

We hear that Mrs. Mallard was standing on the porch of her house with her two small boys when a Yankee rode by with chickens tied to his saddle. In a scornful tone he warned her that the war would soon be over. She defiantly told him that Southerners would fight to the death and that her boys would continue the fight when they were grown.

The Yankees found a hog that Mrs. Mallard had buried. One of the soldiers accidentally discovered that the ground under him was hollow and dug through the roof of the hastily constructed hiding place and unearthed the pig. They butchered the animal right there and rode off with the pig tied to the saddle along with the chickens.

The Mallards now have little to eat.

Saturday, October 1, 1864

The Yankees invaded Doctor Harris's house. They took some pieces of the cake that his cook had made and threw some coins into a plate and rode off.

Shortly after, another band of Yankees approached and took the rest of the cake, as well as the coins left by the first bunch, and ordered Doctor Harris's cook to prepare a meal for them, which they found so delicious they decided to make her come with them back to their camp. Doctor Harris's cook is quite fat and they forced her up on a mule—which she has never ridden in her life. The other Negroes stood around laughing, although, I must admit, I did not see the humor in any of this.

A few hours later the cook came walking back, saying that she fell off the mule so many times that the soldiers decided to go on without her. She told the Yankees that Southern boys would never have taken the money because they were raised with better manners.

Iris said she heard an owl screech near the house, which meant someone would soon die.

Sunday, October 2, 1864

Mr. Garlington has had his Negroes dig new gate post holes. When they ceased work for the evening, he put his bags of gold and silver in the holes and barely covered them with dirt, so that in the morning, unbeknownst to them, the Negroes put the gate post in place without being any wiser. He is quite pleased with himself.

Yesterday morning the Yankees left hurriedly and when they returned at dusk, they had a wounded man with them. They laid him outside by the trellis fence surrounding the garden. He seemed to be in a woeful state. He looked quite parched and, although I assumed his comrades would tend to him, I decided to bring him some water. I approached with great trepidation—there was no one around. He could barely open his eyes and looked as if he were burning up with fever. He was so young, about Tally's age. I showed him the water pitcher and he nodded, which seemed to be quite an effort. I held it to his lips and carefully tipped it so the water trickled into his mouth. Some ran down his face but he drank heartily. When it seemed that he had drunk his fill I stood up, turned, and walked away. "Thank you, Ma'am, from a thirsty man," he called out. I nodded and went back into the house.

When I awoke I looked out the window to see if he was still there. He was gone. Later that morning I saw the soldiers placing his limp body on a cart and taking him away.

I am not as frightened as perhaps I should be

Monday, October 3, 1864

Aunt Caroline learned today that Nora Canning was helped by a kind Yankee. A troop of soldiers drove by her house and stopped. Her youngest was crying and the soldier asked why he was crying. Mrs. Canning said it was because he was so hungry — she hadn't been able to give her children anything to eat for two days. The soldier, his eyes filling with tears, said he would come back later with food. He was as good as his word — returning that night with biscuits and hot coffee, which he shared with her and the children.

Unfortunately, this kind of behavior is rare, and there are daily reports of one horror following another. Mrs. Canning's neighbor was set upon by a band of Yankees who wanted to know how long it had been since our troops passed this way. Her boy refused to tell them and the Yankees tied a rope around his neck and swung him from a tree limb until he was nearly dead. Finally, they cut him down and went on their way, laughing at the wretched joke.

Thus far, we have escaped without such incidents, but I cannot help but wonder if our time will come. We remain as much as possible on the third floor. Aunt Caroline and I do our best to stay clear of the soldiers, who swarm about the house throughout the day.

I am surprised that I am not as frightened as perhaps I should be—certainly not considering our present living conditions.

Lily came down with me to care for Baby Elizabeth while I fixed breakfast. Lily is, as I have said, a great help with the baby. Having Elizabeth here provides a ray of hope that better times than these might be on the horizon.

Wednesday, October 5, 1864

The Yankees laugh at our Negroes because they have not run off the way so many around here have. They fail to comprehend the reason for their loyalty, which the Yankees consider foolish. Amos replied to one, with the air of dignity he always has about him, that he does not leave because this is his home. He is proud of all we have taught him. Iris told them that if she left there would be nobody to take care of Miss Emma. I have known Iris all my life, and I do not know what I would do if she left.

Thursday, October 6, 1864

Lily has come down with scarlet fever. She was very restless all last night, and the fever continues hot and high today and her throat is generally swollen and sore. She is sitting up and talking, which is a good sign, and she remains quite sensible. Colonel Davenport has been kind enough to have one of the Yankee doctors look at her.

Saturday, October 8, 1864

Lily seems relieved this morning. The fever appears to have subsided, although Aunt Caroline insists she remain in bed. She misses being with Baby Elizabeth, but there is too much risk involved. We are all crowded up here in these rooms and it is quite difficult. I am finding it nearly impossible to find the time required to maintain my diary. I strive to wake at dawn, take my diary from the bottom of the bureau drawer, and write as much as I can before breakfast. I feel fortunate that the soldiers have not chosen to search our rooms. We have so little up here and are so clearly in strained circumstances that I do not think the soldiers pay us any mind.

Cousin Rachel sleeps all day and is up all night, which was quite disturbing at first, but I have become accustomed to it.

It takes a long time to recover from scarlet fever and Aunt Caroline is giving Lily as much care as possible.

I have not been able to write Tally and, alas, I have not heard from him in quite some time.

Sunday, October 9, 1864

Mrs. Broyles spent most of the morning looking for her hair comb. She is very pale and is losing a great deal of weight.

Doctor Harris's cook was found dead this morning. Presumably, her heart gave out.

Tuesday, October 11, 1864

Lily seems to be responding to treatment and appears to be on the mend. She rested last night and slept soundly for the first time since the fever began, although she still does not have much appetite, which is fortunate because we have so little to eat. Aunt Caroline is fearful that the baby will also fall prey to the fever.

There was death shining in his eyes

Friday, October 14, 1864

Mr. Garlington has been found hanging from his apple tree. We are all horrified.

At first, it was thought to be a suicide, which apparently was the intent. Foul play was suspected because his shirt was so awkwardly buttoned, and the shoes he had on were new with not a scratch or hint of dirt on the soles. It was discovered that he had been smothered in his bed and only then carried and hanged from the apple tree.

All the silver, jewelry, and money—including the gold hidden under the newly placed gate posts—was taken. It appears that they had been planning this insurrection for quite some time. Mrs. Garlington is beside herself with fear and grief. She is fortunate that she too was not slain, for it is known far and wide that she is quick to whip her servants for the slightest indiscretion.

Romeo is believed to have led the plot and he

has run off, along with the rest of the Negroes. It is said that they rubbed pepper on the soles of their feet, and that is why the dogs cannot locate them.

Mrs. Garlington says she heard nothing.

Father has always disagreed with the way Mr. Garlington treated his Negroes. Mr. Garlington claimed that they were obstinate by nature, and it was required that the impudent ones constantly be reminded of his authority by daily corporal punishment. Fear of their master was, according to Mr. Garlington, necessary to get them to work properly.

Mr. Garlington sold Romeo's wife and oldest child three years ago, which was the cause of grave and continuous problems. He steadfastly refused to let Romeo visit his wife, even though he knew the family to whom she was sold. They did not know the whereabouts of the oldest child.

This was, I know, something Father tried successfully to avoid and he counseled Mr. Garlington to reconsider — which he refused to do.

That same year Romeo's baby son died, although I am not sure what was the cause.

Mr. Garlington accused Father of pampering our Negroes and warned him that it would lead to their becoming indulgent and spoiled, which would in turn lead to insubordination. Both Father and Mother could be quite firm and strict when it was warranted — Father especially — but I think the wisdom of their way can be readily seen in the continued loyalty of our Negroes, while all around us others are running off to join the Yankees or worse, as witness the events at the Garlington house.

Iris has insisted on sleeping outside my room to protect us — which has made her the object of great scorn from the soldiers who are stationed downstairs. They question why she would do this, and Iris tells them that she has nursed me since I was a baby and that she has no intention of abandoning me now. Bless her.

I am proud that our Negroes have chosen to remain with us. I have always wondered what they truly thought. We live with them but we know so little about them. I have often made note of the fact that they are one way with us and another with their own color. I would think that this deception is something they have had to adopt.

I must confess that whenever I saw Mr. Garlington I had the eerie feeling that there was death shining in his eyes. Perhaps all of this was written in the book of fate.

Sunday, October 16, 1864

All around us people are leaving. Some heading south, others heading west, taking whatever they can with them. I support Aunt Caroline in her decision to stay. Where would we go, and what would happen to us? We cannot go to Richmond, for all reports are that the situation there is dire. And what would happen to our beautiful home? How would Father and Tally find us?

How precious life is

Saturday, October 22, 1864

All hope is slipping away. I pray that God will sustain us, yet, at times, I feel it would be better if we all would die and put an end to this misery. I try not to let thoughts like that enter my mind. I think of seeing Father and Tally again and that gives me strength to continue. I think of how Mother would have liked me to act and that too gives me strength.

Tuesday, October 25, 1864

At night we can hear the guns in the distance breaking the silence, and during the day we fear that Colonel Davenport and his men will leave and abandon us to the lawless soldiers who are roaming the countryside. Having our home taken over by Colonel Davenport has proved to be a blessing. If it were not for his protection I do not know what would become of us.

Saturday, October 29, 1864

My thoughts are of Tally. Is that bad? I wonder if we would be happy as man and wife. Marriage is such a holy state, and I would not want to enter it unless it were to remain so.

This war has made me see how precious life is. Odd when I am surrounded by death and darkness. I fear I have wasted my youth on trivialities where sugar plums and balls achieved a disproportionate importance, along with the craving for useless objects. I was living in a state of ignorant bliss. Well, this is no more.

Tuesday, November 1, 1864

Cousin Rachel continues to be a trial. Aunt Caroline has had to have a stern talk with her about how she acts when she is around the Yankee soldiers. Aunt Caroline is concerned that Cousin Rachel might provoke them to something regrettable. I heartily agree with her, and I am not sure why Cousin Rachel is acting this way.

We no longer talk about anything—although I have tried. Early yesterday morning I heard her softly playing her flute while I was washing. I quietly reentered the room and waited until she had finished the piece. It was quite nice, which I told her. She just stared at me with a faraway look in her eyes and then got back into bed, turning her face to the wall.

Aunt Caroline and I have been appreciative of the manner in which the soldiers who occupy our house have conducted themselves and wish the situation to remain so. We expected the worst after hearing reports from others. We have not been shown any disrespect, and they show much consideration.

Despite their kindness I cannot help but think how long it has been since I lay down in peace at night. I sleep fitfully and wake in the morning just as tired as when I laid my head on the pillow the night before, fearful of what the day will bring.

Why can we not go on living as we did before?

Thursday, November 3, 1864

Cousin Rachel is filled with hatred for the Abolitionist soldiers, and she says the war has turned her heart to stone. She says the Yankee flag is a horrible symbol of this hateful invasion. She has sewn a small Confederate flag inside the folds of her dress. She says this is the true spirit we should show, and she accuses me of putting on a false face when the enemy is all around us. I have always been a very private person and I cannot change my ways now. Cousin Rachel accuses me of superficiality, which, I must confess, offends me. I do have faith — although at times, Lord knows, I waver — that better days are coming. I am sorry this irritates her so, but I could never abide political talk and I am afraid I cannot do so now. Even before the war, when Father and Mr. Garlington and Doctor Harris would talk about politics at the dinner table, I usually found some reason to excuse myself.

I do not know whether secession is the right choice, nor do I know if freeing the Negroes will answer all our problems. They seemed so content before all this began that I am unsure as to what all the fury is about. Why can we not go on living as we did before? Is it not enough to believe in the life we had? I do not hate the Yankees as Cousin Rachel does but nor do I understand why they have chosen to come to our land and spread terror, deprivation, and upheaval in their wake.

Friday, November 4, 1864

Cary Baldwin and her children have left.

Mrs. Baldwin heard someone at the front door and before she could put some clothes on, they were thundering at the shutters, demanding entrance and waking the few Negroes that remained.

All were ordered to assemble in the dining room. The children, rudely awakened by the commotion, were dumbfounded by all the activity.

She and the children were driven into a state

of panic. The Yankees have incited the remaining Negroes into a fearful state—employing them to keep watch and let them know of any suspicious activity, such as Confederate soldiers or hidden weapons.

She begged the soldiers to conduct themselves with more consideration, explaining that she had not been well lately and that she feared the excitement might damage her health. One of the Yankees—who appeared to be quite drunk—told Mrs. Baldwin, in a surly tone, that her husband and brothers were killing his countrymen and that they did not care what happened to her.

She was afraid that he would kill her, but he was more interested in food than anything else, and he ransacked her house with the others and took what food they could find, shot all the pigs and fowl, and rode off, carrying them in bags.

I fear my heart will simply break

Monday, November 7, 1864

Colonel Davenport and his soldiers departed, hurriedly, this morning, although we are unsure of the cause.

The house is in a complete shambles.

The downstairs is in wretched condition. It is frightening to see. There is dirt and confusion everywhere. They have broken into everything — chests and bureaus forced open, their contents destroyed or taken, the china and the crystal shattered, and the fruit knives Mother prized gone. The linens and curtains have been torn; the furniture destroyed; the piano in the parlor broken, I fear, beyond repair.

Outside, our lovely lawn is no more — there are ruts made by their wagon wheels criss-crossing every which way, and Mother's garden has been trampled by their horses and mules, who have also stripped the bark from the trees in the apple orchard. Most distressing of all is that they have taken our horses — the stables are empty except for Falla's colt — and have butchered most of the animals and taken them too. The smokehouse lock has been pried open, the door forced in, and the contents emptied. The yard is filled with rotting garbage.

The Negroes' houses remain intact.

I immediately began trying to restore order in the pantry and the kitchen, with help from Iris and Denise. It will take days and, I fear, many of the other downstairs rooms are beyond repair. The library remains, oddly, untouched. I think this is due to the fact that Colonel Davenport used the library as his office and also because the Yankees have no interest in books.

I wonder if these few words can convey my despair. I fear that nothing I say can truly express it. For the first time in quite a while I have shed tears. I fear my heart will simply break.

Friday, November 11, 1864

Early yesterday a group of Yankees came by but, much to our relief, passed on without coming into the house.

Saturday, November 12, 1864

Still no Yankees. We do not know what to expect.

Sunday, November 13, 1864

Last night three Yankees came looking for our soldiers and the guns they said they had heard we had hidden. I was awakened by the sound of their horses' hooves on the back porch. They were banging on the back door with their sabers and threatening to break in unless we responded. Fortunately, Aunt Caroline was able to rush downstairs in time to prevent any more damage to the house. She barely had time to put on her night dress and her hair was falling loosely around her shoulders. Aunt Caroline explained that the house had been occupied these past two months by Colonel Davenport, who only recently departed, and that we were sure, therefore, that there were no troops hiding about. This seemed to assure them—although they remained sitting all over the front porch and laughing and joking in the most outrageous manner all night. Finally, at dawn, they rode off.

Thursday, November 17, 1864

Nelson, along with almost all the other Negroes except Iris and Amos, has run off. I am sure he convinced the younger ones to go with him. We are all quite dismayed. Fanny, Rosetta, and the children all left with him. I am certain that Nelson convinced them to do that. Nelson's leaving has taken me quite by surprise, I must confess. Amos and Iris remain as faithful as ever.

Sunday, November 20, 1864

We walk about in constant fear of the Yankees, fearing that at any moment we might be invaded. We all feel like prisoners in our own home, although there is no one about. We are afraid to open the windows or step outside. Sometimes

I feel so shut up I have to go out for a walk despite the weather and the fear. When I do, Aunt Caroline insists that Amos be nearby.

I am no longer young

Wednesday, November 23, 1864

Sometimes I try to remember what our lives used to be like, but it has been so long I have difficulty conjuring up the images. I can, at times, picture the house when it was alive and full of activity — everyone getting ready for a carriage ride into town or perhaps an excursion into the countryside. Mother giving the servants last-minute instructions, Father and Brother Cole seeing to the bags, and me sitting at my vanity for what I am sure must have seemed like endless hours, holding everyone up while I decided how I should wear my hair or which dress would be the most flattering. Those days are gone forever — I am no longer young.

At times I feel like I am a thousand years old — that is what this cruel war has done to me. No matter what the outcome — if peace was declared tomorrow, if the Yankees vanished from our land and allowed us to govern ourselves, if all the Negroes were somehow miraculously returned to us and resumed their former roles, if all of this were to occur, I know I have changed forever and there is no going back.

I was at a loss for words

Thursday, December 1, 1864

Cousin Rachel has become impossible to understand. She says she feels like a heroine because of the war and the Yankees, who, she believes, are certain to be driven from our land. She wishes she could play a greater role in their defeat. Women, she says, should be proud of the task that is before them and that in the end we can all be proud that we have stood up to the Yankee invaders. She says she is sorry she does not have a pistol, for if she did, she would shoot some Yankees.

I cannot share her view and wonder if there is something wrong about me. I scold myself for my despair, but I am certain that Cousin Rachel is simply deluding herself. She lives in a world of make-believe.

Friday, December 2, 1864

This morning, while looking out my window, I saw a Yankee soldier standing just behind the oak out by the garden. He stood still, as if he knew I was watching, but I could see the brim of his hat when he made a movement. I was concerned about it all day but nothing ever came of it.

Saturday, December 3, 1864

We wait in breathless anticipation for news.

Sunday, December 4, 1864

Baby Elizabeth is ill.

She has a very high fever and sleeps little, tossing in her crib. She eats nothing, and swallowing seems to cause her great pain.

Aunt Caroline is besides herself with concern. She stayed up with her until early this morning, when I awoke and went in and gently urged my aunt to get some sleep, assuring her that I would wake her if necessary.

The baby slept peacefully for a few precious hours and, at dawn, opened her tiny eyes. I think

I could see a questioning look in her eyes, wondering where her mother was. I was at a loss for words to comfort her and had to be satisfied with patting her cheeks.

We both must have fallen back to sleep, for when I awoke I was sitting in the rocker with the baby fast asleep in my arms.

Monday, December 5, 1864

Baby Elizabeth still has a raging fever and shows little appetite. Her throat appears to be swollen and it is quite distressing to see an innocent child suffer so. No matter what kind of nourishment we give her she turns her head aside. It is as if she too has given up hope.

How long O Lord, how long?

Thursday, December 8, 1864

The weather turned quite cold today. O how I long for the time when there was a fire in every hearth shielding us from the cold nights, when the house was such a haven from the harsh winter just outside our door.

The moon always seemed to shine most brilliantly in the winter, hanging in the night sky like a hopeful light among the twinkling stars. At those times it seemed that all was well.

Now the house is constantly damp and cold. There is little firewood and, although Amos has done his best to keep us supplied, he is old and tired and can only do so much. We are huddled in blankets and shawls a great deal of the time.

Friday, December 9, 1864

I scarcely think the baby will live out the night, as her fever is once again making rapid progress.

She seems quite ill despite our constant attentions, which I fear are proving futile. I try to keep my faith in the Lord, but I'm afraid not even He can help us.

We are all alone. Thank the Lord for Amos and Iris. Amos has provided enough wood for a fire, which helps keep the baby warm. Without them we would be in an even worse state.

Sunday, December 11, 1864

How long O Lord, how long?

Wednesday, December 21, 1864

I have not written in my diary for the past two weeks, being simply unable to record the tragic death of my dear cousin, who was taken so suddenly from us. We have lost the only ray of light in our dreary existence. This war has torn apart our lives and the pieces have been scattered to the wind. The only thing that keeps me from utter despair is the knowledge that Aunt Caroline needs me in the way that I needed her when

Mother left us forever. I cannot fail her and must put my unspeakable grief aside.

Thursday, December 22, 1864

I am growing thin and feeling weak. I can no longer even weep.

There is a black hole where my heart previously beat

Sunday, December 25, 1864

How many thousands of years ago was it that we all came together to celebrate this most joyous holiday?

But this day is forever cloaked in a black shroud of grief.

There is a black hole where my heart previously beat. Anything would be better than this painful wound—a wound that grows infinitely more acute when it is filled with the uncertainty about Father and Tally. I am unwilling to accept that they, along with Mother, Brother Cole, Uncle Benjamin, and Baby Elizabeth are gone forever—never to return.

I find it impossible to imagine them lying cold upon some battlefield with no one to care for them. I cannot bring myself to believe—as others seem to—that somehow it would be worth it. Is anything worth dying for? Is this awful waste—this painful sacrifice—justified in God's eyes?

Epilogue

Miraculously, Emma's house, although extensively damaged, survived the war. Aunt Caroline and Amos Braxton continued to live there when the war ended. Aunt Caroline, forced to earn a living for the first time, turned the house into an orphanage. Amos, although seventy-one, was an accomplished carpenter and he was able, along with some hired help, to repair the inside of the house. "Aunt Caroline's Home," as it came to be known, functioned from 1865 until 1893, when Aunt Caroline died at the age of sixty-two. Amos died three years later.

Cousin Rachel lived with her mother at the orphanage, helping occasionally with the children, but only occasionally. Although speculative, it is assumed that Rachel Colsten suffered a nervous breakdown during the war.

In 1867, Aunt Caroline was forced to commit her to the Richmond Lunatic Asylum, where she died a year later when she fell, jumped, or was pushed from the fourth floor of the asylum. Unfortunately, the available information surrounding her death is confusing and, at times, contradictory.

Colonel Robert Stiles Simpson died at the Battle of Cedar Creek on October 19, 1864. Apparently, he had become separated from his regiment, was without a coat in bitter cold weather, and had taken the overcoat of a dead Yankee soldier for warmth. He then attempted to find his way back to his own lines and was accidentally shot and instantly killed by Confederate soldiers, who mistook him for the enemy. He is buried next to his wife, in the Simpson family graveyard, which survives to this day. The house, however, went to ruins after Aunt Caroline's death and was demolished some time after 1893. There is no trace of it today.

Taliaferro "Tally" Mills was wounded twice and taken prisoner on the outskirts of Winchester, Virginia, in September 1864. He was taken to a Federal prison in Elmira, New York, in April 1865, when Confederate commander General Robert E.

Lee surrendered the Army of Northern Virginia to Union commander General Ulysses S. Grant at Appomattox Courthouse, ending the war.

He was released a month later and made his way back to Virginia and the Simpson home where he was united with a relieved Emma Simpson, who knew nothing of his capture or his fate. They moved to Richmond where they were married. Tally went to work for *The Richmond Examiner*, beginning what was to become a lifelong, successful career as a journalist. In his later years he became well known as the publisher of a small but influential weekly newspaper. They had two children, Robert, born in 1868, and Jane (named after Jane Eyre), born two years later.

During the early years of their marriage, Emma, who was considered quite a beauty, taught piano and volunteered at the Richmond Library. Over the years, as the children grew, she devoted more and more time to working at the library, where she developed a reputation as quite an authority on Charlotte Brontë. Tally died in 1916, at the age of seventy, and Emma died the next year.

Iris, who, with her daughter, Dinah, accompanied Emma and Tally when they moved to Richmond, lived with and worked for them for a number of years. Some time before 1875 Iris married and moved north with her husband and daughter, possibly to Chicago. Their whereabouts after that are unknown.

The ring Tally sent Emma never did quite fit on her finger — she always wore it on a chain around her neck. It has been passed down through the generations and currently is worn on the finger of her forty-five-year-old great-great-granddaughter Emma Clark Broughton, who lives in New York City, where she is a journalist.

Life in America
in 1864

Historical Note

Any understanding of this nation has to be based . . . on an understanding of the Civil War. . . . The Civil War defined us as what we are and it opened us to being what we became, good and bad things. And it is very necessary, if you're going to understand the American character in the twentieth century, to learn about this enormous catastrophe in the nineteenth century. It was the crossroads of our being, and it was a hell of a cross-roads: the suffering, the enormous tragedy of the whole thing.

—Shelby Foote

The Civil War, fought between 1861 and 1865, was the darkest and most critical period in American history. It was a bloody, brutal, and bitter war. Three million soldiers fought at a time when the population numbered only thirty-one million.

More than six hundred thousand died—nearly as many Americans as died in all other wars combined—two-thirds of them from illness and disease. Frequently families were torn apart as brother fought brother.

There were two central issues that divided the nation and caused the war to be fought. One was slavery. The economy of the Southern states was based on slavery. In the 1850s, as the country was rapidly expanding to the West, the issue of slavery in the new territories became, despite attempts at compromise, an incendiary issue.

Many Northerners were opposed to the expansion of slavery in these new territories. Abolitionists, an extreme but vocal minority in the North, wanted to abolish slavery wherever it existed. They considered it evil and contrary to the ideals of democracy.

Most citizens of the South believed that blacks were biologically inferior to whites and therefore unable to care for themselves. Blacks were better off, they argued, being watched over by their white masters. Northerners, they believed, were out to destroy their way of life both economically and socially. Southern leaders threatened to secede from the Union and form their own country. They claimed that the United States was a voluntary Union of independent states that had a right to withdraw from that Union at any time. The majority of citizens in the North favored preserving the Union. This, along with slavery, became the primary reason the war was fought.

In 1860 Abraham Lincoln was elected president. He vowed to keep the country united: "A house divided against itself cannot stand. I believe this government cannot endure permanently half slave and half free. I do not expect the Union to be dissolved—I do not expect the house to fall—but I do expect it will cease to be divided. It will become all one thing, or all the other."

For Southern leaders, Lincoln's election signaled that the time had come for drastic action. Eleven Southern states seceded from the Union, creating the Confederate States of America.

In December 1860, Southern forces, supported

by artillery, surrounded the tiny federal Fort Sumter, located on an island in Charleston Harbor, South Carolina. By the spring of 1861, Lincoln was forced to send ships to resupply the Union soldiers who had been besieged for over four months. On April 12, 1861, the Confederates opened fire on Fort Sumter and the Civil War began.

Both sides were tragically mistaken in their belief that the war would be brief.

The first major battle took place just twenty-five miles away from Washington, D.C., near a small stream in northern Virginia named Bull Run. Ordinary citizens brought picnic baskets and binoculars and sat down to watch the fight from the sidelines. The Confederate soldiers counterattacked so fiercely that the watching civilians and the inexperienced Union soldiers fled in terror. Almost five thousand soldiers were killed or wounded that day.

For the next four years the war was a series of endless, bloody battles in places like Shiloh, Cold Harbor, and Antietam. In three days of fighting at Gettysburg there were over fifty thousand casualties. Americans were slaughtering each other at a staggering rate and it seemed that the war would never end.

The North and the South were two very different regions. The population in the North was about twenty-two million, while the South had only nine million inhabitants, at least three million of whom were slaves. The North was industrialized and had a well-developed transportation system, while the South was mainly an agricultural society. Three-fourths of the world's cotton was grown in the South. It was a vital part of the Southern economy — and cotton picking was dependent on slave labor. The South had a much stronger military tradition than the North, but they were badly outnumbered and outgunned.

Militarily, the South's only goal was to repel what they considered the invasion from the North. They had the advantage of fighting on familiar terrain and the benefit of local support. However, this meant that Southern civilians suffered greatly as the war ravaged their land and destroyed their way of life. The Union Navy's blockade of the coastline resulted in constant shortages of food, clothing, and medical supplies.

Almost every Southern family lost at least one family member during the war.

On the first day of January, 1863, President Lincoln signed the Emancipation Proclamation, which stated that all slaves in the Confederate States were now free. This did not have much practical effect, since the South was not about to pay attention to a document issued by the enemy. But it did have great political impact because it officially declared that the war was being fought to put an end to slavery as well as to preserve the Union.

By 1864 the Confederate army, commanded by General Robert E. Lee, had been weakened by battle losses. General Ulysses S. Grant, who commanded the Union armies, pressed his advantage, attacking Lee in Virginia. Their ensuing battles resulted in massive casualties on both sides. Still, a decisive victory eluded a determined Grant, and Lee maneuvered successfully and continued to rally his troops to fight on.

Hoping to increase the pressure on Southern soldiers and civilians, Grant sent General William T. Sherman's one hundred thousand-man army eastward to Atlanta, Georgia. After seizing Atlanta and leaving it in flames, Sherman began his "March to the Sea." His men burned and destroyed nearly everything in their path as they advanced relentlessly to Savannah, up into North Carolina and on to Virginia to join Grant.

In Virginia, Grant's siege of Petersburg eventually forced the evacuation of Richmond, the Confederate capital. Lee had no choice but to face the military reality that the Southern cause was lost. He surrendered to Grant at Appomattox Courthouse, Virginia, on April 9, 1865.

Tragically, only five days later, President Lincoln was assassinated. He never saw the Thirteenth Amendment, which abolished slavery forever, signed into law.

A typical Southern plantation home.

Slave quarters.

The fashions of the 1860s were very ornate. Dressmakers often copied Parisian designs they found in illustrated magazines such as these. Southern girls and women wore fanciful silk-and-satin dresses with crinolines (to maintain the full skirt) to balls and other social gatherings.

Girls wore specially designed costumes with narrower skirts for horseback riding. They sat sidesaddle, which was considered more ladylike.

JANE EYRE.

An Autobiography.

EDITED BY

CURRER BELL.

IN THREE VOLUMES.
VOL. I.

LONDON:
SMITH, ELDER, AND CO., CORNHILL.
1847.

The title page from the first edition of Jane Eyre. One of the most popular English writers of the nineteenth century, Charlotte Brontë was also read in America during the Civil War. She published under the pseudonym Currer Bell—a man's name—because at that time in history, critics and readers often dismissed women's writing as inconsequential.

Photographer Alexander Gardner captures a scene of daily life.

Abraham Lincoln was president of the United States from 1861 until his assassination in 1865. His primary concern was the preservation of the Union. Before his inauguration, he said there would be "no bloodshed unless it is forced upon the government."

The second draft of the Gettysburg Address written in Lincoln's own hand. Beginning with the famous words, "Four score and seven years ago, our fathers brought forth on this continent a new nation, conceived in Liberty and dedicated to the proposition that all men are created equal," it is only about two hundred seventy words long and captures the reasons the war was being fought.

Thousands of boys who fought in the Civil War were between the ages of twelve and sixteen. Many of them recorded their experiences in journals and diaries.

The Civil War was the first American war to be documented with photography. When pictures of the dead at Antietam Battlefield, like the one shown here, first arrived at Mathew Brady's New York City studio, The New York Times reported, "Mr. Brady has done something to bring home to us the terrible reality and earnestness of war. If he has not brought bodies and laid them on our dooryards and along the streets, he has done something very like it. . . ."

Telegraph battery wagons such as this one near Petersburg, Virginia, made it possible for journalists to report on the war. It was not uncommon for people to learn about the deaths of loved ones from the newspapers.

Weeping Sad and Lonely (When This Cruel War Is Over)

Words by Charles C. Sawyer. Music by Henry Tucker.

CHORUS
Weeping sad and lonely,
Hopes and fears how vain!
(Yet praying,)
When this cruel war is over,
Praying that we meet again!

VERSE 2.
When the summer breeze
is sighing
Mournfully along;
Or when autumn leaves
are falling,
Sadly breathes the song.
Oft in dreams I see thee lying
On the battle plain,
Lonely, wounded, even dying,
Calling but in vain. (Chorus)

VERSE 3.
If amid the din of battle,
Nobly you should fall,
Far away from those
who love you,
None to hear you call,
Who would whisper
words of comfort,
Who would soothe your pain?
Ah! the many cruel fancies
Ever in my brain. (Chorus)

VERSE 4.
But our country called you, darling,
Angels cheer your way;
While our nation's sons are fighting,
We can only pray.
Nobly strike for God and liberty,
Let all nations see,
How we love the starry banner,
Emblem of the free. (Chorus)

Though this song originated as a Union lament, the sorrow expressed in the lyrics was felt by people on both sides. The South soon adopted it and altered it to say, "Oh! how proud you stood before me / In your suit of gray, / when you vowed to me and country / Ne'er to go astray."

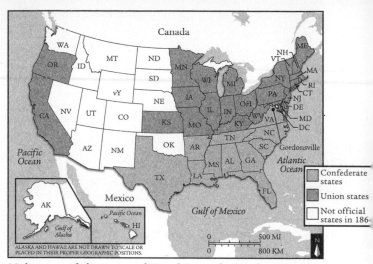

Modern map of the continental United States, showing the approximate location of Gordonsville. This map also shows which were Union states and which were Confederate.

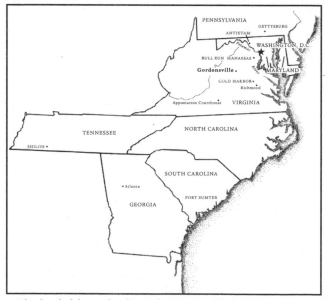

This detail of the South indicates the important battles of the Civil War.

170

About the Author

Barry Denenberg is an acclaimed nonfiction writer whose main interest is American history. Writing for the Dear America series was compelling to him because, "It allowed me to write history from the perspective of those who experienced it. Not the history made by politicians, but the history made by ordinary people during extraordinary times. History from the bottom up, not the top down." Denenberg immersed himself in a wealth of material, concentrating on the diaries and letters of the time, sources not generally available to middle-grade readers.

"The Civil War was a pivotal event in the history of the United States. It was the only war where Americans fought each other. Because the military activity took place overwhelmingly in the South, I decided to tell the story from the Southern perspective, a perspective that asks the question — as moving today as it was then — What is it like to have your world torn apart while war rages at your doorstep?" Setting the diary in Gordonsville, a small town in Virginia, enabled him to show the grave effects of the war on ordinary civilians.

"While doing the research for *When Will This Cruel War Be Over?*" he says, "I found I could, after a while, *almost* feel what it was like to be Emma Simpson. It is that experience that I hope comes through in her diary."

Mr. Denenberg's nonfiction books include *An American Hero: The True Story of Charles A. Lindbergh*; *Voices from Vietnam*, a Booklist Editor's Choice Book and an ALA Best Book for Young Adults; *The True Story of J. Edgar Hoover and the FBI*, a Junior Library Guild Selection; *All Shook Up: The Life and Death of Elvis Presley*; and *Nelson Mandela: "No Easy Walk to Freedom,"* all published by Scholastic. *When Will This Cruel War Be Over?* was his first work of fiction for middle-grade readers. He lives in Bedford, New York, with his wife, Jean, and their daughter, Emma.

Acknowledgments

The author would like to thank the editorial, production, and design staffs
at Scholastic for their painstaking efforts on his behalf. In particular, Tracy
Mack, whose caring shines through on every page.

Grateful acknowledgment is made for permission to use the following.

Cover portrait by Tim O'Brien.

Cover background: Grant's Great Campaign — Steven's Battery at Cold
Harbor, Library of Congress.

Page 163 (top): *The Old Westover House* by Edward Lamson Henry, 1869, oil on
paperboard, 11 1/4 x 14 5/8 inches, accession number 00.11, Gift of the
American Art Association, The Corcoran Gallery of Art, Washington, DC.

Page 163 (bottom): Slave cabins, Library of Congress.

Page 164 (top): Ladies' fashion, winter 1866, North Wind Picture Archives,
Alfred, Maine.

Page 164 (bottom): Horseback riders. Wood cut, ibid.

Page 165 (top): Title page of *Jane Eyre*, published by Smith, Elder and Co.,
Cornhill, 1847, London.

Page 165 (bottom): The house of Mrs. Lee in Pleasant Valley, Maryland,
Gardner's Photographic Sketch Book of the Civil War, Dover Publications, Inc.,
Mineola, New York.

Page 166 (top): Abraham Lincoln, photographed by Matthew B. Brady, from
Mr. Lincoln's Camera Man: Matthew B. Brady, ibid.

Page 166 (bottom): The Gettysburg Address, Library of Congress.

Page 167: Edwin Francis Jennison, private in a Georgia infantry regiment,
ibid.

Page 168 (top): Dead soldiers in front of Dunker Church at Antietam, ibid.

Page 168 (bottom): U.S. telegraph battery wagon, ibid.

Page 169: Music and lyrics to "Weeping Sad and Lonely (When This Cruel
War Is Over)," from *Songs of the Civil War*, Dover Publications, Inc., Mineola,
New York.

Page 170 (top): Map by Jim McMahon.

Page 170 (bottom): Map by Heather Saunders.

Other books in the Dear America series

DEAR AMERICA

The Diary of Abigail Jane Stewart

The Winter of
Red Snow

Valley Forge, Pennsylvania, 1777

KRISTIANA GREGORY

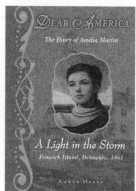

DEAR AMERICA

The Diary of Amelia Martin

A Light in the Storm

Fenwick Island, Delaware, 1861

KAREN HESSE

DEAR AMERICA

The Diary of Piper Davis

The Fences Between Us

Seattle, Washington, 1941

KIRBY LARSON

DEAR AMERICA

The Diary of
Remember Patience Whipple

A Journey to the
New World

Mayflower, 1620

KATHRYN LASKY

DEAR AMERICA

The Diary of Lydia Amelia Pierce

LIKE THE
WILLOW TREE

Portland, Maine, 1918

LOIS LOWRY

DEAR AMERICA

The Diary of Clotee, a Slave Girl

A Picture of
Freedom

Belmont Plantation, Virginia, 1859

PATRICIA C. McKISSACK

DEAR AMERICA

The Diary of Margaret Ann Brady

Voyage on
the Great Titanic

RMS Titanic, 1912

ELLEN EMERSON WHITE